Flappy Investigates

Also by Santa Montefiore

Meet Me Under the Ombu Tree
The Butterfly Box
The Forget-Me-Not Sonata
The Swallow and the Hummingbird
The Last Voyage of the Valentina
The Gypsy Madonna
Sea of Lost Love
The French Gardener
The Italian Matchmaker
The Affair
The House by the Sea
The Summer House
Secrets of the Lighthouse
A Mother's Love
The Beekeeper's Daughter
The Temptation of Gracie
The Secret Hours
Here and Now
Flappy Entertains
An Italian Girl in Brooklyn

The Deverill Chronicles

Songs of Love and War
Daughters of Castle Deverill
The Last Secret of the Deverills
The Distant Shores

Santa Montefiore

Flappy Investigates

**SIMON &
SCHUSTER**

London · New York · Sydney · Toronto · New Delhi

First published in Great Britain by Simon & Schuster UK Ltd, 2022

1 3 5 7 9 10 8 6 4 2

Simon & Schuster UK Ltd
1st Floor
222 Gray's Inn Road
London WC1X 8HB

Simon & Schuster Australia, Sydney
Simon & Schuster India, New Delhi

www.simonandschuster.co.uk
www.simonandschuster.com.au
www.simonandschuster.co.in

A CIP catalogue record for this book
is available from the British Library

Hardback ISBN: 978-1-3985-1073-9
Trade Paperback ISBN: 978-1-3985-1074-6
eBook ISBN: 978-1-3985-1075-3
Audio ISBN: 978-1-3985-1077-7

Typeset in Bembo by M Rules
Printed and bound by
CPI Group (UK) Ltd, Croydon, CR0 4YY

*Dedicated to my dear friend Nicole Majdalany
with love and gratitude for the countless times
she has made me laugh.*

Chapter 1

Badley Compton, Devon, 2010

If there was one thing Flappy abhorred, it was people poking their noses into other people's business. It was beneath one's dignity to invade someone's privacy and something Flappy would never *ever* do – unless it was absolutely necessary and, by all accounts, unavoidable. Now was one of those moments.

Careful not to catch her pale cashmere sweater on the brambles, Flappy crouched in the bushes, binoculars in hand, and focused her attention on the young couple standing in the garden of Hollyberry House, in front of a dead apple tree. The woman was pretty with shiny brown hair and a slim, willowy figure, dressed in clothes that Flappy would describe, with a slight curl of her upper lip, as 'bohemian'. The husband was of average height, bald with glasses, wearing a suede jacket and jeans. These people had clearly moved down from London hoping to find a bucolic paradise here in

Badley Compton. Well, Flappy didn't blame them. Badley Compton was undeniably very charming. With its quaint little harbour full of blue-bottomed fishing boats, Georgian townhouses, old-fashioned cafés and bookshop, and the close-knit community one didn't often find in this modern world of constant coming and going, it was a townie's idea of rural bliss. And Flappy was the unrivalled queen of it. If it weren't for *her* there would be no summer fêtes, jumble sales, Harvest Festival teas, Halloween parties, book clubs and May Day dances to bring the community together. It was all the doing of the redoubtable Flappy Scott-Booth, not that she would *ever* take the credit. Flappy was, to her core, both gracious and charitable. However, when these two upstarts from London had had the audacity, the sheer nerve, to occupy Flappy and Kenneth Scott-Booth's front pew at church on Sunday, the very seats they had sat in for almost thirty years, Flappy's graciousness and charity had been stretched to their limit. Something had to be done.

Flappy watched the couple closely. She couldn't hear what they were saying. In spite of being good at practically everything, she was not good at lip reading. She focused the binoculars on the tree and imagined they were wondering whether or not to cut it down. Flappy, were they to seek expert advice, would suggest they train a climbing Himalayan rose up it. She had one at Darnley and it was quite spectacular. In fact, when she and Kenneth opened the gardens, the *many beautiful* gardens, of Darnley Manor to the public for three weeks in June, the rose inspired both admiration and awe from visitors who came from far and wide to view it. The Himalayan rose at Darnley was, to be sure, one of the wonders of Badley Compton.

Flappy shifted the binoculars further and ran her critical gaze over the borders. Poor *poor* things, she thought with a swell of *Schadenfreude*, which, had she been aware of it, would have made her feel quite ashamed. However, Flappy was conveniently *un*aware of the less gracious and charitable side of her nature. The gardens of Hollyberry House were truly an overgrown mess and needed a great deal of work to put right. She sighed at the couple's misfortune and considered how incredibly lucky *she* was to have a small army of gardeners at Darnley who kept the borders, lawns, arboretum and orchards at their luscious best. She wondered who this unfortunate pair were going to employ to untangle the terrible jumble of bindweed and elder that plagued their new home. She sniffed and lowered her binoculars. One thing was clear. This young couple were here and they were here to stay.

Flappy staggered out of the bushes onto the lane and smoothed down her trousers. Just as she did so, a familiar yellow Volkswagen came into view. Mabel, Flappy's best friend and unofficial lady-in-waiting, was stooping over the steering wheel concentrating very hard on the road. When she saw Flappy, she checked her rear-view mirror and, seeing no one on her tail, pulled up. She rolled down the window. 'Flappy!' she exclaimed, noticing the binoculars at once. 'What *are* you doing?'

Flappy lifted her chin and gave Mabel a superior smile, as if surprised that Mabel couldn't tell because, really, it was very obvious. 'Birdwatching, Mabel,' she replied. 'I've just spotted an extremely rare long-tailed skua, not to be mistaken for the pomarine skua. It's easy to muddle them up.' Flappy, in truth, had no idea what either looked like but had heard two twitchers from Norway discussing them on the local news a few days before. If there was one thing Flappy was good at, it was fishing information out of her memory when information was required. Indeed, she had an exceedingly good memory and this was a prime example of how very good it was.

Mabel was duly impressed, albeit a little confused, as to why Flappy would be birdwatching in town. Didn't bird watchers, on the whole, head out to the beach or country-side? Nevertheless, she certainly wasn't going to question her friend, who always knew best. 'Do you want a lift?' she asked.

Flappy climbed into the passenger seat. 'I left the Range Rover at the pub,' she explained.

Mabel giggled. 'If anyone sees it, they'll think you're having a mid-morning beer.'

Flappy frowned. 'I don't think so, Mabel.'

'No, of course not. You're absolutely right. If there's one person in Badley Compton who *won't* be having a beer in the pub, it's you, Flappy.' Mabel was keen to please her friend and, as Hollyberry House was just behind the hedge, her memory was triggered. 'You remember that couple who sat in your seats at church on Sunday?'

'They're not *our* seats, Mabel,' said Flappy, pretending that she hadn't minded.

'Well, not officially, but everyone knows that's where you and Kenneth always sit.'

4

'What about them, this couple?' Flappy's gaze drifted out of the window in search of the long-tailed skua to demonstrate her uninterest.

'They've just moved down from London. They lived in Bloomsbury. He's some sort of computer expert and she's a journalist. They've got two young children called Martha and Rafe.'

Flappy did not trust computer experts or journalists and gave a sniff, which signalled her disapproval. 'I gather they've moved into Hollyberry House,' she said breezily. 'Apparently the garden's a jungle. Perhaps I should send one of my gardeners round to give them some advice. That would be nice, wouldn't it?'

'Oh, it would,' Mabel agreed.

'It would be nothing for me but mean so much to them.'

'You're very generous, Flappy. I'm sure they'd really appreciate the gesture.'

'I'll get onto it right away.' Flappy squeezed her eyes shut. 'Their name has just escaped me,' she added, which wasn't true because Flappy never forgot anything.

'They're called Price. Jim and Molly Price,' Mabel replied. '*She* was in Big Mary's this morning having coffee on her own. I noticed she only had coffee. I suppose one doesn't get a figure like that without abstaining from croissants and cake.'

'Young people,' said Flappy with a sigh. 'The lovely thing about getting older is that one doesn't have to worry about one's weight anymore. I eat like a horse, as you know, Mabel. There are more important things in the world to worry about than one's figure.'

Mabel drew up outside The Bell and Dragon. 'Shall I pop round later?' she asked eagerly, for Mabel enjoyed the status of Flappy's Number One Friend, with the special privilege of being permitted to turn up at Darnley uninvited.

'Actually, today I'm having tea with Hedda. Why don't you come for mid-morning coffee tomorrow and bring the ladies? We need to plan the New Year's Eve ball.'

'Ball? I thought it was a party,' said Mabel. The New Year's Eve party had been an annual event in the town hall for years.

'It's going to be a ball and *I'm* going to host it,' said Flappy, who had only just this moment thought of it.

Mabel's eyes lit up. 'Oh, Flappy! What a marvellous idea.'

'I know,' said Flappy with a self-satisfied sniff. If Hedda Harvey-Smith could give an end of summer party that dazzled the local community then *she*, Flappy Scott-Booth, could do even better. 'A grand ball such as Badley Compton has never seen.'

'Well, Hedda and Charles's party was pretty spectacular,' Mabel reminded her. They had, after all, invited Monty Don and hired Jason Donovan to perform.

'Mine will be even more so,' said Flappy determinedly, and Mabel was in no doubt that it would be.

Flappy stepped out of the car. As she walked away, Mabel gazed at her with envy and admiration. There she was, in her sixties, with the slim figure of a much younger woman. Mabel took in the beautifully cut trousers, the cashmere sweater that matched her aquamarine eyes, her perfectly coiffed blonde bob and the angular line of her jaw and cheekbones, which rendered Flappy's face so striking, and sighed at the miracle of such effortless beauty. Mabel was a poor imitation, but still she tried so very hard to copy her friend. Flappy was unaware, because Mabel fell short in every area of her endeavours, but had she noticed she would have been pleased. After all, is it not true that imitation is the highest form of flattery?

Flappy drove home listening to Dolly Parton. Had she had company in the car she would have played something classical like Andrea Bocelli, but as she was alone she sang along contentedly to 'Jolene', liking the sound of her own voice very much. In fact, had she lived a different life, a life with less responsibility and less Kenneth, she might have been a singer.

At last she turned into the stately gates of Darnley Manor and drove up the tree-lined avenue towards the house. Through the trees Flappy could glimpse the garden where gardeners in green T-shirts and khaki trousers could be seen trimming the yew hedges and cutting back the shrubs, for now autumn was beginning to settle onto the leaves in soft yellows and browns and the odd flash of red. Every time Flappy saw the house she felt a deep sense of satisfaction and gratitude, yes gratitude, because she considered herself so *so* lucky to have such a superior-looking home.

Darnley Manor was indeed what one would describe as an 'important' house. Not quite stately, but jolly close. It was built in the eighteenth century, which was incredibly chic, and remodelled a hundred years later, adding large, airy rooms to the back with big latticed windows that looked out onto the croquet lawn where Flappy held her parties. The house had charm due to the harmony of its proportions and the great age of the stone, the colour of wet sand and clothed in wisteria, which flowered an exquisite purple in the spring.

She pulled up on the gravel, beside her husband Kenneth's caramel-coloured Jaguar, and climbed out. With a light gait, because Flappy was in a very good mood, she skipped up the steps to the front door and flounced into the hall. No sooner had she entered than Kenneth, short and stout, appeared at the top of the stairs in a pair of red trousers and a blue shirt, straining slightly over his belly, having changed out of his golfing clothes. 'Ah, just the person I want to see,' he said.

'Hello, darling. How was golf?'

'Bloody dog ran off with my ball!'

'I thought dogs weren't allowed on the course.' The course to which Flappy referred was, of course, the Scott-Booth Golf Course, which Kenneth built when the couple had first settled in Badley Compton some thirty years before. Immaculate, manicured and expensive, it was Kenneth's pride and joy and Flappy's saviour, for what wife wants a husband at home all the time?

'Damn thing escaped from someone's car.'

'How very careless of the owner. I hope you complained. People shouldn't be allowed to behave like that.'

'I was going to complain until I discovered who the dog belonged to.'

'Who?' Flappy's attention was now piqued, because Kenneth was the sort of man who made no distinction between a duke and a dustman. After all, he had come from nothing and made his fortune with a fast-food chain that he had subsequently sold for a great deal of money. Flappy, on the other hand, noticed every subtle nuance in class and status. She wondered who Kenneth considered important enough to warrant their dog having permission to tear about the course.

'Colin Montgomerie,' Kenneth declared.

Flappy rolled her eyes. 'The golfer?' *Good Lord,* she thought with disappointment, *I was expecting a royal at the very least!*

'The big man himself. I couldn't tell *him* to take his dog off the course, could I? Even though the damn thing was charging about the green with my golf ball in his mouth! Now if he'd dropped it into the hole that would have been another matter.' He chortled as he came down the stairs. 'Now, I've just been speaking to Jasper and guess what?' He raised his eyebrows and grinned.

'What, our son's finally earning enough money not to have to ask us to top up his bank account?'

'Not this time. He and Briony are moving to ...' Kenneth hesitated, hoping to create a sense of drama, but he only succeeded in irritating Flappy, who did not like her daughter-in-law, who she considered upwardly mobile and pretentious. 'Badley Compton,' he announced in triumph.

Flappy looked appalled. 'What? Coming here? To live?'

'Well, not right here, not to Darnley, but they're going to rent a house in town. Isn't that good news? They're arriving next week, which means they'll be here for Christmas!'

'That's a bit sudden.'

'They've been planning it for some time, apparently.'

'Then why didn't they give us notice?'

'They're spontaneous, Flappy. That's what Antipodeans are, you know. Spontaneous.'

'Queering my pitch, that's what *I* call it.'

'It'll be nice to have one of our children living in the same country as us for a change.'

Shame he can't leave his wife in Australia, Flappy thought. But she was careful not to say that out loud. Flappy was, above all else, a woman with exceedingly good manners. 'It's wonderful news,' she exclaimed brightly, because if there was one thing Flappy was good at, it was playing the Glad Game when the Glad Game needed to be played. 'Let's go and have lunch,' she suggested. 'I've just discovered who has moved into Hollyberry House. Come and I'll tell you all about them.'

'Does the husband play golf?' Kenneth asked hopefully, following her into the kitchen.

'I would say not, darling. He looks like the sort of man who would be more at home in a fashionable bar in Soho with a dry Martini than on the third hole with a golf club. He's going to be frightfully disappointed with Badley Compton. We're not fashionable down here. Jim and Molly Price *are*.' And Kenneth knew very well that fashionable was, according to his wife, 'very common'.

After lunch Persephone, Flappy's twenty-eight-year-old personal assistant, returned from her lunch break, which she had taken on one of the garden benches, enjoying the early autumn sunshine and the sound of birds. Flappy had employed her at the end of August to lessen her load, because being all things to all people was hard for one woman to accomplish, even a woman like Flappy, who was a master at multitasking. Persephone was sweet-looking, with brown hair and brown eyes and a sprinkle of freckles over her nose. She was gentle and kind, efficient and honest, but most importantly she was discreet. Flappy abhorred gossip almost more than she abhorred anything, at least when it was about *her* – a teeny bit of gossip about other people was permitted when it was absolutely necessary. Persephone was not a gossip and that was one of the reasons Flappy warmed to her. She knew that whatever the girl heard or saw at Darnley would not be passed around the community. With Persephone she was safe. Hadn't Persephone proved herself recently, after discovering Flappy in a romantic clinch with Charles Harvey-Smith at the Harvey-Smiths' end of summer party? Indeed, Flappy knew she could count on Persephone to keep her mouth shut, when a shut mouth was required.

'Right, Persephone, we have work to do,' said Flappy, striding into the library where Persephone's desk had been set up in front of the window.

Persephone smiled. 'You haven't taken on anything else, have you, Flappy?' she said, calling her boss by her first name. After said romantic clinch, Flappy had insisted they do away with all formality. She had confessed her affair to Persephone on the drive home from the party and in so doing had raised her status from PA to confidante. With her daughters in Canada and Australia and therefore unavailable to share her trials, Flappy was very happy to share them with Persephone.

'I have. A teeny little something, but nothing you and I

can't handle. After all, we're an unbeatable team, aren't we? I'm going to throw a New Year ball.'

'Goodness, what a wonderful idea!'

Flappy was pleased that Persephone shared her enthusiasm, but not surprised. That was another reason she had taken her on. Persephone had a refreshing 'can do' attitude, just like Flappy herself. An admirable quality. One of Flappy's finest. 'It must be spectacular. Magical. The kind of ball that people talk about for years. The sort of event they tell their grandchildren about when they pick out the best moments of their lives.'

'How exciting!' Persephone gushed.

Flappy narrowed her eyes. 'We need a theme.'

'Isn't New Year itself a theme?'

'We need something more original. Something beyond. It can't just be New Year like everyone else's New Year. We must add something unique.' Flappy stilled her busy mind, as she always did when she needed to concentrate, and, lo, in popped a brilliant idea. 'A masked ball,' she exclaimed. 'A *Venetian* fancy dress ball.' She envisioned herself in a magnificent dress, inspired by the great Venetian painters of the Renaissance, and smiled with satisfaction. 'Yes, *un ballo in maschera,*' she said, because, among Flappy's many other talents, was, of course, a gift for language. '*Che meraviglia!*'

Persephone was excited. She too liked the idea of dressing up in a beautiful gown. 'Then the tent must be Italian-inspired.'

'It must look like Venice,' said Flappy, warming to the idea. 'With a canal and a bridge. Can it be done?'

'It'll cost you, but I'm sure we can find someone to do it.'

'Splendid. What a fine way to spend one's money.' Flappy knew Kenneth would agree. He, more than anyone, loved a party.

'Leave *me* to do the research,' said Persephone, opening her notebook and writing *Flappy's ballo in maschera* in big letters at the top of the page. '*You* need to do the guest list.'

Flappy's eyes were gleaming as her busy mind ran with the idea. 'We will spare no detail. There will be golden goblets on the tables and twinkling stars on the ceiling and gondolas on the canal. Perhaps we can hire some Italian *gondolieri* to mingle with the guests in their stripy shirts and hats with red ribbons. *Molto chic, no?*'

Persephone, who spoke fluent Italian, Spanish and French, smiled at Flappy's Italian, because she knew how limited it was. Not that anyone else could tell. As far as Flappy's friends were concerned, she spoke the melodious Italian of Dante. 'Badley Compton won't know what's hit it,' said Persephone.

'*Tal quale*, just what I was thinking,' said Flappy.

At four on the dot, because Flappy was punctilious about being on time, she drove her shiny grey Range Rover through the gates of Compton Court, Mozart's 'Queen of the Night' playing very loudly on the CD player in case anyone happened to be listening. Charles and Hedda's grand Georgian home came into view at the end of the long, sweeping drive. It was, Flappy had to admit, magnificent. In order not to feel jealous – because jealousy was unbecoming in a woman who was blessed with every material comfort – Flappy reminded herself that Compton Court did not have a swimming pool. The swimming pool at Darnley was, it must be said, a rather splendid feature being simultaneously indoors and outdoors by virtue of one wall being completely made of glass. At the touch of a button the glass folded away and, lo, in tumbled the fresh air and sunshine. Flappy reflected hard on the swimming pool as she parked her car in front of the classical façade.

Johnson the butler opened the door and showed Flappy into the drawing room. 'I will let Mrs Harvey-Smith know you are here,' he said, leaving her alone to admire the artwork on the walls and the photographs in silver frames on the occasional tables. Flappy was meticulously tidy, Hedda was not. The room had a pleasant, relaxed feel to it. There were magazines strewn across the coffee table, objects and trinkets cluttered on the surfaces, and cushions that didn't conform to any specific colour scheme arranged haphazardly on the sofas and armchairs. It was a very English drawing room, Flappy thought, and an aristocratic one at that. After all, Hedda was the niece of a marquess. As Flappy reminded herself of her new friend's pedigree she felt her competitiveness ebb away, because Flappy couldn't compete with aristocracy nor could she help being impressed by it – there was something about a title that made her feel strangely submissive. It was a relief, this feeling, because if there was one thing Flappy abhorred, it was the game of one-upmanship; it was so tiring maintaining her position on top.

Flappy was about to take a seat when Charles's face appeared at the glass of the door to the terrace. Flappy caught her breath. He was impossibly handsome with thick grey hair, a long straight nose, a sensual mouth and the most startling green eyes she had ever seen. Really, they were absurdly green, like jade. Her initial reaction on seeing him there was one of excitement. How she had adored those afternoons making love in the cottage in the grounds of Darnley Manor.

'Beauty!' exclaimed Charles, striding into the room. He looked like he was dangerously close to embracing her. Oh, how Flappy longed to be embraced. To be enfolded in those strong arms and kissed by those soft pillow lips.

She moved away like a startled doe. 'Hello, Charles,' she said demurely, caging with the greatest force of will the beast inside her that only a couple of weeks ago had been rampant and free.

'You look ravishing.'

'Thank you,' she replied, edging behind the sofa as he took another step towards her.

He frowned. 'Aren't you going to greet me, Beauty? Don't I deserve a kiss? Come now, why so coy suddenly?' He lowered his voice. 'Just one.'

'Charles, it's over,' she hissed, eyeing the door anxiously, knowing that Hedda would walk in at any moment.

Charles grinned mischievously, something she had once loved about him, but now it filled Flappy's heart with trepidation. 'It'll never be over, Beauty. You're under my skin. I think of you every moment of every day. Love isn't something you can just turn off like a tap.'

'It wasn't love, Charles. You know that.'

His grin turned lascivious as he ran his eyes over her

15

body, greedily devouring every inch of her. 'You're right. It was lust, too. Delicious, dangerous lust. Remember how I brought you to such great heights of pleasure?' Flappy most certainly did and her cheeks flushed crimson. 'You couldn't get enough of it. Don't pretend you've forgotten. We can do it again.'

Flappy heard footsteps in the hall. She lifted her chin and in her most commanding tone said, 'No, Charles. You must behave. Hedda is my friend and I will *not* betray her.'

At that moment Hedda walked in as Flappy knew she would. Hedda gave Charles the sort of reproving look one might give a misbehaving child. 'Are you being annoying, Charles?' she said. 'Sorry, Flappy.'

'Well, I'll leave you ladies to it,' said Charles, not remotely contrite. 'Lovely to see you, Flappy. If I didn't know better, I'd think it was spring.'

Flappy sighed with relief as he left the room. 'Hedda,' she said, embracing her.

'Flappy. Come and sit down. We have much to discuss. Tell me, have you found out who that couple are who sat in your and Kenneth's seats in church on Sunday? I'm dying to know.'

Chapter 2

'What are we going to do about it?' Hedda asked, biting into a chocolate brownie. Flappy refrained, although they did look delicious.

'Of course, I don't mind them sitting in our seats on the odd occasion,' Flappy lied, taking a sip from her china teacup. Fine bone china. The best. Must have been inherited, she thought with approval. 'But I don't really want them sitting there *every* Sunday.'

'They need to be told,' said Hedda decisively. 'They can't just move into Hollyberry House and assume a place in the front row of the church. It's presumptuous. Have they no consideration for people like you and Kenneth who have lived in Badley Compton for years?'

'I imagine they consider themselves very important,' said Flappy.

Hedda thought about that a moment as she licked the chocolate off the tips of her fingers. 'Yes, I think they do,' she agreed.

'But we must give them the benefit of the doubt,' said Flappy firmly. 'After all, they wouldn't have known they were our seats, having only just moved here, would they? They might have assumed they could sit anywhere.'

'I'm sure they'll be ashamed when they find out,' said Hedda.

'Of course, they will,' Flappy concurred, enjoying the feeling of being magnanimous. After all, it would not do to be judgemental when passing judgement was something she abhorred in other people. 'They're city folk. City folk have no idea how things are done down here.'

'Then we'll let them know. Gently and kindly, but in no uncertain terms,' said Hedda.

'For their own good,' Flappy added.

'Dinner, here at Compton Court, with you and Kenneth?'

'And Graham,' Flappy suggested. It was always good to get the vicar along on such occasions, to give the event an air of gravitas.

'Good idea, although his wife, what's-her-name, is frightfully dull.'

'Joan. Bread sauce without any salt,' said Flappy. 'Although I never *ever* speak ill of anyone.'

'He's the salt, though, isn't he?' said Hedda, enjoying the metaphor. 'Without him she'd be nothing. But together they're a good team. Yes, a dinner to welcome the Prices into the community. People were so kind when we arrived. That's what's wonderful about Badley Compton. That kind of community spirit is rare these days. I'm sure they'll get the drift.'

'Of course they will,' Flappy agreed, happy to have an ally in this matter. A powerful ally. The niece of a marquess, no less. 'And we'll forgive them and welcome them wholeheartedly.'

Hedda took another brownie off the plate. 'Are you sure you're not going to have one? They're heavenly.'

'They do look delicious,' said Flappy. 'But I have an iron will when it comes to maintaining my figure. If I give in now, my restraint will be broken and then where will I be? Fat and unhappy and not fitting into any of my clothes.' And Flappy *did* have the most beautiful clothes.

Hedda gave a throaty laugh. 'That ship sailed long ago.' She took a bite. 'I'm much too old now to worry about my waistline. If my clothes get too small, I just buy bigger ones. I gave up worrying about my figure years ago and I've never been happier.'

Flappy observed her friend, her sturdy figure, badly dyed brown hair, mumsy clothes and mouth full of brownie, and acknowledged that she was, indeed, happy. Hedda had no airs and graces, no pretences and no desire to be anything other than what she was. Just like Flappy. That's why Flappy liked her so much, because, besides their very different body shapes and sense of style (Hedda had none), and their pedigree, of course (Flappy could not deny *that*), they really were two peas in a pod.

'Why don't you take one for Persephone?' Hedda suggested. 'I'll get Johnson to pop it in a bag. She and George are very sweet together, aren't they?'

'Young love,' said Flappy with a sigh of longing. She really

19

did miss those heady moments of passion with Charles. Her eyes strayed to the door and she found herself hoping he'd come back.

'Yes, young love. They're perfect together. You were so clever the way you engineered their romance.'

'Oh, it was luck, really. If you hadn't invited her to the party, she'd never have seen him again.'

'I know a good thing when I see it and Persephone is right for my son.'

'I agree.'

Hedda rang the bell for Johnson. 'I'll invite the Prices for dinner next week. How does your diary look?'

Flappy's diary was quite empty. Nevertheless, she pulled a face to show how very busy she was. 'Much too full,' she complained with a mournful sigh. 'However, I'll free myself up just this once. I never *ever* cancel a dinner for a better invitation. But this is important. And we need to do it sooner rather than later.'

'I'll say, or they'll squat in your seats and there'll be no getting them out!'

With that horrible thought worming into her brain, Flappy climbed into the car and drove out through the gates into the lane. A short distance from the house she pulled up into a lay-by. So anxious was she suddenly at the thought of the Prices squatting in her and Kenneth's seats in the church *indefinitely* that she took the chocolate brownie out of the bag and stuffed it into her mouth.

The next morning Hedda called Flappy to tell her that dinner with the Prices and the vicar was going to be on Wednesday of the following week. Flappy tapped her fingernail on the open page of her diary where that evening lay empty, and mumbled, 'Well, if I move the meeting to the following morning and bow out of dinner, I should be able to finesse it. Yes,' she said, after a contemplative pause, 'I can do it, Hedda. How kind of you to arrange it.' Then she wrote *Dinner, Compton Court* in her diary in ink.

Flappy glided through the rest of her week feeling very benevolent towards the Prices. They'd accepted Hedda's invitation to dinner and, according to Mabel, left a very large tip in Big Mary's tip jar after Jim devoured not one but *two* of her lemon cream slices. They must be good people, she thought to herself as her mind sought the odd respite from being extremely busy.

However, when Sunday morning came around again, she wasn't going to leave anything to chance. 'Kenneth darling, do get a move on. We should get to church early today,' she exclaimed, standing at the bottom of the stairs while her husband straightened his tie in the mirror on the wall at the top. Kenneth was very pleased with his tie for it was the official Scott-Booth Golf Club tie which Flappy had designed especially for the members. Peony pink and emerald green stripes on a navy-blue background. The height of chic and flamboyance, just like Flappy herself. Kenneth lifted his chin, smoothed down the few hairs that remained on the crown of his head, and went down to join her.

'If you're worried about the whatever-they're-called sitting in our seats again—'

'Prices,' said Flappy.

'You needn't worry. I'm sure Graham will steer them into one of the pews at the back.'

'We cannot count on Graham. He's a man of God and in God's eyes all men are equal.' Flappy strode out to Kenneth's Jaguar. 'I'm not going to rely on Graham,' she said, opening the car door. 'At times like this, one can only rely on oneself.'

Kenneth climbed in beside her and started the engine. The Jaguar emitted a low murmur, like a growl. They set off down the country lanes into town and Flappy, who normally adored the turning leaves and ripe autumn light, could think of nothing else but her precious seats at the front of the church and the danger of losing them.

They arrived fifteen minutes early. Flappy gave a sigh of relief when she saw that only a few very old people were walking slowly up the path towards the church. Fashionable people like the Prices would never arrive early, she thought with satisfaction; their seats were safe.

Flappy wandered at a leisurely pace, taking pleasure now from the golden leaves on the horse chestnut trees and the warm amber sunshine that illuminated the path before her. How she loved autumn. The wistfulness of it, the sweet melancholia, the delightful sense of change that lingered in the air as summer finally gave way, in fits and starts, to the new season of mist and mellow fruitfulness. Ah Keats, she mused, what a master of words was he, *close bosom-friend of the maturing sun.*

On entering the church, she saw, to her relief, that those who had already arrived were sitting in their usual seats. Her pew, her and Kenneth's, was empty and waiting for her to lay claim to it. Never had she been so happy to see it. Without further ado, and leaving Kenneth talking to old Mr Bartley who kept the graveyard tidily mown, she went and sat down.

'You're here early,' said Graham, when he appeared in his robes to greet his congregants.

'I wanted to have a little peace and quiet to contemplate this beautiful church and those lovely flowers,' Flappy said, nodding at the somewhat woeful arrangement that Esther Tennant had placed in the alcove in front of her. Flappy made a mental note to tell her. After all, as chairwoman of the Badley Compton Church Committee, the responsibility for church flowers fell onto *her* broad shoulders. There was a rota and a standard and Esther had fulfilled only *one* of those requirements.

Soon the church began to fill with locals. After the tenth person had told Flappy how surprised they were to see her in her seat so early, she was beginning to lose patience. But Flappy was a woman with deep reserves and she just smiled and replied, with a touch of piety, 'Spending a few extra minutes in God's house is so good for one's soul, don't you think?' And those impertinent congregants retreated to their seats filled with admiration for the fine example that Flappy set.

Just before the service was about to start, long after Kenneth had taken his place beside his wife, the big door at the back opened and the sound of whispering swept down

23

the aisle like an unwelcome wind. Flappy turned round to see who had come in so late and to show her disapproval. Being late for church was a definite no-no. 'So sorry,' hissed Molly Price, not looking sorry at all. Taking one of her young children by the hand, she proceeded to march down the aisle, towards the front row. Flappy smiled to herself, because she and Kenneth were firmly planted in their seats. There was no danger of them being usurped. She was sure Graham would direct them to the back of the church where there would doubtless be empty seats for newcomers like them.

However, Graham was, as Flappy had so accurately observed, a man of God, and in God's eyes all men – and women – were equal. As the quartet clattered loudly down the aisle (Flappy observed with a flush of disapproval that Molly Price was wearing high heels), Graham smiled a warm, welcoming smile and directed them to Flappy and Kenneth's pew. 'You don't mind squeezing up, do you?' he asked.

'Not at all,' said Kenneth in that genial way of his that instantly made people like him. Flappy, however, hesitated; being liked was not important now. Could they not see that the pew was shorter than the others due to a buttress in the wall? There simply wasn't room for four more people. But Graham had already anticipated this and, without much ado, placed two kneeling cushions in the front for the children so that Molly and Jim could settle into the pew beside Flappy.

Flappy was *not* amused. If the truth be told, she was absolutely furious. There she was, in the pew she had sat in for over thirty years without having to share it, because quite frankly anyone could see that there wasn't space for more than two to sit comfortably, being made to make herself very small and *un*comfortable on account of an insensitive pair of arrivistes. However, if Flappy was good at one thing, it was disguising her wrath when wrath was best disguised. She smiled sweetly as only she could and shuffled along so that she and Kenneth were pressed against each other like a pair of love birds. Molly thanked her, but Flappy perceived a lack of conviction in her words and, in its place, a sense of entitlement, as if she believed her family had a right to be there. Jim sat down without regarding the two people he had inconvenienced. The children plonked themselves down on the kneeling cushions and, to Flappy's horror, began to play games on the iPads their mother gave them, presumably to keep them quiet. Flappy looked across the aisle to see that Hedda, sitting in the front pew with Charles, was just as appalled as she was.

They had clearly misjudged the Prices.

The service was ruined for Flappy, who did not like sitting so close to Molly or having to endure the sight of her two children engrossed in a most mindless pastime when they should have been sitting quietly, listening to the vicar. There were plenty of other children in the congregation who were behaving like little paragons of virtue. *Townies*, Flappy thought disparagingly. Materialistic and indulged because their selfish parents were much too busy being upwardly mobile. Country children were, on the whole, unspoilt and obedient. Flappy inhaled through her nose and out through her mouth, concentrating hard on the meditation practice her Indian guru Murli had taught her. *Breathe in peace and calm, breathe out negativity.* It was a challenge and one she was not sure she was mastering. There was simply too much negativity around her to allow peace and calm in.

At the end of the service Flappy was unable to contain her outrage a moment longer. She stood up to leave. But before she did so, she smiled at Molly. However, the steeliness in her eyes could not be disguised, even by a master of concealment. 'Such a shame your children missed out on the service,' she said. 'We who have lived in Badley Compton for almost thirty years are very proud of our church and vicar, who is the best example of his kind. I'm sure you'll discover, when you've settled in, that he has much wisdom to impart. And children, with their fertile young minds, benefit from wise seeds planted early.' *There,* Flappy thought triumphantly, *firmly put in her place.*

But Molly simply returned her smile and replied breezily, 'If my children had not been distracted by their iPads, I can assure you that neither you nor I would have heard a word of his wisdom.' And with that she swept past Flappy and headed out of the church, followed by her two children and her husband, who wandered slowly after her, his attention on his phone.

Flappy was speechless, which was quite something for a woman who prided herself in always having the last word. She turned to her husband. 'Did you hear that, Kenneth?'

'I did,' he replied.

'The nerve,' she hissed.

But Kenneth chuckled in that easy-going way of his. The chuckle of a man who was only rattled when a dog ran off with his ball on the golf course. 'I'm grateful to those devices. I'd have been very put out if I hadn't been able to hear Graham's sermon.'

'Oh, Kenneth!' said Flappy in exasperation and she went to find Hedda, whom she knew she could count on to agree.

Hedda was suitably outraged. 'I'm rather wishing I hadn't invited them for dinner,' she said.

'The battle is just commencing,' said Flappy, fired up now and ready to fight for that last word. 'This was a preliminary skirmish.' She narrowed her eyes. 'Together we are a force to be reckoned with, Hedda. We cannot abide people with that kind of attitude in this town. We cannot allow ourselves to be taken over. It is not in my nature to judge or condemn, but I'm afraid they have overstepped the mark.'

'What shall we do?'

'Kill with kindness, Hedda. And if that doesn't work, we'll bring out the artillery.'

'What's the artillery?'

'The artillery, my dear Hedda, are the decent people of Badley Compton.'

'Of course,' said Hedda, feeling a little better. That was another wonderful thing about living in a small, close-knit community. One could count on people's support. 'Well, I'd better go and introduce myself,' she added, setting off down the aisle.

'Chin up, Hedda,' said Flappy and, she wanted to add, *you are the niece of a marquess,* but Hedda was already striding out into the sunshine.

'Hello, Flappy.'

Flappy would recognize that chocolatey voice anywhere. 'Charles,' she said, and those green eyes, so deep and beautiful like a lagoon, bore into her as they had done during many secret afternoons in the cottage. She caught her breath, struggling to maintain control. 'Wasn't that a lovely service?' she said.

'You're looking radiant, Beauty,' he murmured, tracing the angles of her face with devotion.

'You mustn't call me that,' she reminded him softly.

'You know I don't like to do as I'm told.' That mischievous grin again.

Flappy grew weak. She glanced about the church, afraid of being overheard. 'I'm well aware of that, Charles. But over really does mean over and as much as you try to persuade me to change my mind, my mind, once set, is unchangeable.'

'You have not factored in my heart, Beauty. You still have it. It's like a little bird in your hand.'

'Oh, Charles.'

'You can't pretend that you feel nothing for me.'

'My feelings for you could never be enough to warrant jeopardizing my marriage or, for that matter, my friendship with Hedda. I'm sorry, Charles, but no means no.'

'I won't give up,' he said, but Flappy was now hurrying down the aisle towards the door. There was a teeny part of her that swelled with pleasure at the sound of those words, said with such determination and longing. *I won't give up.* Flappy considered herself a woman unafflicted by the sin of pride, but she had to admit, quietly and only to herself, that she was, really, very pleased to be desirable still.

The following morning Flappy met Mabel in Big Mary's for a cup of coffee. This was unusual. Flappy only ever went into Café Délice if she wanted something from Big Mary, like catering for one of her teas, or to subtly extract information, for the café, positioned so pleasantly overlooking the harbour, was the hub of Badley Compton where everyone who was anyone met and shared the local gossip. What Big Mary didn't know wasn't worth knowing.

They were joined by Esther Tennant, Madge Armitage and Sally Hancock, the core of Flappy's court. But this wasn't an entirely social meeting. Flappy had business to attend to. 'I'm the first to welcome newcomers,' she said, sipping her espresso and ignoring, smugly, the plate of cakes in the middle of the table which the other ladies were blithely devouring. 'But the ingratitude of this couple beggars belief. It's not just about the seats in church; I mean, what sort of person would I be if I minded about front-row seats?' She laughed to show how great the distance was between that sort of person and herself. 'It's the presumption. How could they allow their children to play computer games while Graham delivered such a rousing sermon? How could they?'

The women were in complete agreement, which was where Flappy liked them to be. 'I couldn't believe my eyes when I saw them marching down the aisle,' said Sally, shaking her curly red hair. 'There was plenty of room at the back.'

'Very insulting to poor Graham,' said Madge, taking a lemon cream slice off the plate and sinking her teeth into it with a sigh of pleasure.

'He's so patient, though. I'm sure he didn't mind,' said Esther. A sharp look from Flappy induced her to add, 'But it's unforgivable to treat a vicar with such disrespect, and high heels in church is a real faux pas. She made such a racket marching down the aisle I thought someone had let the horses in.'

Flappy nodded. If there was one thing she abhorred, it was high heels, *anywhere*. High heels, she maintained, were very common.

'What are you going to do about it?' asked Mabel, because Flappy could always be relied upon to put things right when they were so clearly wrong.

'That's what I want to talk to *you* about,' she said, looking at each woman in turn. 'You are the artillery, ladies. We may need you.'

'We?' asked Madge.

'Me and Hedda. The Prices are going for dinner at Hedda's on Wednesday, and Kenneth and I are invited. We're going to embrace them into the community. Gather them up. Make them feel welcome. Once included, they will learn how things are done around here. It's really very simple. If one doesn't take trouble with people, they get up to all sorts of nonsense.'

'They go rogue,' said Esther firmly.

'Quite,' agreed Flappy. 'If we allow them to sit in the front row in church, where will they plonk themselves next?'

Mabel looked horrified. 'They'll take over everything,' she said in a quivering voice.

'We can't have them doing that!' exclaimed Madge, licking her fingers.

'Do you think they'd do that?' asked Esther, who wasn't quite convinced by Flappy's argument.

'You give people an inch and they'll take a mile. That Molly is a steely-looking woman. She'll be running everything by Christmas, mark my words. If we don't put a stop to it now, she'll have won over the whole town and it'll be *her* book clubs and *her* parties and *her* fêtes you'll all be going to.' Flappy narrowed her eyes. 'I know her sort. Strong-minded city women who like to be on top.'

But there was only room in Badley Compton for one person on top, and Flappy was not budging.

At the thought of Molly Price taking her throne, Flappy eyed the cakes anxiously. Then she took one. A big, moist slice of chocolate cake. As the flavour overwhelmed her senses, her fear of being usurped melted away and all she could think of was whether it would look greedy to eat the entire slice. Flappy abhorred greed almost as much as she abhorred rudeness. However, she bit off a little more and then a little more until the whole slice was gone. As she wiped her mouth with a napkin, she considered her empty plate. She had *had* to finish the cake. It would have been rude not to.

Chapter 3

Ever since Flappy had ended her brief affair with Charles and run back to Kenneth with her heart full of remorse, Kenneth had slept in Flappy's bed. He, of course, had no clue as to why his wife had suddenly invited him back after eight years of being relegated to his dressing room, or why she'd started calling him 'Toad' again, a term of endearment that had been left in the past to gather dust, along with sex, romance and all the other exciting things that pertained to young love. But he wasn't going to look a gift horse in the mouth; Flappy had welcomed him back and that was all he needed to know.

Flappy's eyes had been opened. Years of domesticity and intimacy had done away with the magic and yet, she realized now, love endured. True love, deep love, the sort of love she felt for Kenneth. It didn't matter that he snored. Well, that wasn't entirely true. She *endured* it with loving patience, the grunting and groaning, heaving and gurgling, and turned her mind to other things, like her New Year's Eve ball.

Sex, on the other hand, was a different matter. However

loving her heart, sex was something Flappy did *not* want to endure, at least not with her husband. Nonetheless, one cannot invite a man into one's bed and expect him to roll over and go to sleep. Kenneth was a man like any other. Sure, he was obsessed with golf and that game, so tedious and dull according to Flappy, had done her the very great favour of taking his mind off sex and tiring out his body, so that when it came to bedtime he was much too exhausted to even attempt a foray. However, now he was back in her bed, temptation defeated exhaustion. There she was, lithe and beautiful and smelling of bath oil, and Kenneth was unable to resist. He was her Toad again. He put out a hand and placed it on her hip, and Flappy was too polite to remove it.

Sex with Charles had been out of this world. Not even Toad at the height of his toadery could compete with the sheer sexual prowess of Beastie. Beastie had had a gentle touch, a slow, unhurried pace, a full and sensual kiss. Indeed, he had taken Flappy to great heights of pleasure, heights to which Toad could never dream of taking her. Love was love, but sex was a thing apart that didn't rely on love to fuel or enhance it; it had a life of its own. Flappy could vouch for that.

The truth was, even though Flappy loved Kenneth, he just didn't cut it in the bedroom. However, if Flappy was good at one thing, it was being resourceful. She discovered that she could take some pleasure from the experience by closing her eyes and pretending Kenneth was Charles. It didn't always work because Kenneth's touch was a bit rough, his kisses too wet and his pace too quick. But there were moments, rare to be sure, when Flappy would sigh and moan and arch her back, and then, with a sharp intake of breath, a gasp and a sigh, her cheeks and chest would flush pink and a wave of delicious pleasure would break inside her and spread throughout her entire body like a flood of warm honey. Kenneth would stare at her in amazement, pleased and proud that he had managed to do that for her, her Toad, who had never induced such an orgasm in his wife even in the early days of their marriage.

The result was that Kenneth now had a swagger in his walk. The swagger of a man who has rediscovered his sexuality, and in so doing found talents and abilities he hadn't known were there. His golf game improved. He moved more fluidly and swung his club more gracefully. His balance was steadier, his confidence swelled, and the little white ball rolled time and again into the hole just as he wanted it to. By some miracle, Kenneth believed he had become a good lover. The toad had become a prince. Who'd have thought it?

As long as Flappy felt guilty about having betrayed him, Kenneth would be welcome in her bed and *endured*. She had behaved badly, after all, and if the odd night of sex was her penance, then she would gladly tolerate it. However, she wouldn't feel guilty for ever, perhaps up until Christmas, and then Kenneth would be encouraged to return to his dressing room and Flappy would have the bed to herself once more. How she looked forward to that.

The night before Hedda's dinner party, Flappy and Kenneth were lying in bed side by side. Flappy had encouraged him to consume a few extra glasses of claret, a little ploy she had devised for making him too sleepy for mounting, and so he was making his way slowly through *Golf Monthly*, eyes drooping and head nodding. There would be no hand on her hip tonight. Flappy was reading the new novel by Charity Chance, her favourite romantic writer, who just happened to be the pseudonym of her dear friend Sally Hancock. A secret pleasure she did not admit to anyone, not even Kenneth, who failed to notice that she had slipped it into the jacket of Arundhati Roy's *The God of Small Things*. She was beginning to feel a teeny bit aroused as the hero was spreading the heroine's legs and tracing his tongue up her inner thigh, when the telephone rang.

She looked at the clock on her bedside table. It was well after ten. Who on earth had the impoliteness to call at *this* hour? She picked up the phone. 'Darnley Manor, Flappy Scott-Booth speaking,' she said in an irritated tone of voice. Kenneth sat up with a start and wondered which of their four children was in trouble. 'Jasper? Really, darling, it's awfully late. Can this not wait until morning?'

'It *is* morning where I am,' came the reply.

Flappy sighed. 'Your father and I are in bed.'

Jasper laughed. 'We're leaving for London today,' he told her.

Flappy stared at Kenneth in alarm. 'Today? When will you land?' She knew it took a very long time to fly from Australia to London, but not long enough. They'd be in Badley Compton in a few days.

'On Friday. I've arranged for a people carrier to drive us to Devon.'

'A people carrier? How many are you?'

'Just us and the boys, but Briony has so much luggage.'

Flappy's jaw tensed. 'I'm sure she does.'

'We're really looking forward to seeing you.'

'Me too,' said Flappy, sensing she was being buttered up. If there was one thing Flappy was good at, it was detecting when she was being schmoozed.

'Can I have a quick word with Dad?'

'He's a teeny bit busy,' said Flappy, knowing now what her son was after and visualizing with resentment Briony's many suitcases filled with clothes that Kenneth had paid for.

'I thought you said you were in bed?'

'We are. He's asleep.'

'Just a quick word, Mum. I know he won't mind and it's kind of important.'

Kenneth put out his hand. Flappy passed him the phone.

'Hello, Jasper. How much do you need?'

Flappy was unable to sleep, which was rare. Like everything else, Flappy was good at sleeping. However, Jasper's request for money had made her blood boil. She couldn't understand why he couldn't get a proper job. His father had started his own business when he was only twenty-five and, with hard grind and determination, had turned it into an empire of fast-food emporiums, which had mushroomed on every high street in the country. One could be tempted to say that Jasper had no ambition because he wasn't hungry like his father had been. Kenneth had grown up in a leaky house in a poor community north of London; Jasper had been raised in a mansion in a prosperous town in the south. But Jasper's younger brother, Daniel, worked for a sports management company in California and was making lots of money. The truth was that Jasper had no ambition because he was made like that, and nothing was going to change if Kenneth continued to fund him. Jasper would protest, of course. He called himself an 'entrepreneur', but the only thing he'd ever done was start up a bespoke gifting company and Lord only knew what had become of that. Flappy wondered what he was going to do in Badley Compton. Then, as that worry turned into a very great fear – because, what would everybody think? – she found she really couldn't sleep at all and went downstairs to raid the fridge. Raiding the fridge was something Flappy never *ever* did, except in exceptional circumstances. This was one of those moments. She put a piece of bread in the toaster, took down a jar of peanut butter from the cupboard and waited for the bread to toast.

In spite of a headache and gritty eyes, Flappy got up at five, as she did every morning, and padded down to the swimming pool and gymnasium. She did not normally swim, not because she didn't enjoy the feeling of cool water against her skin, but because she did not like doing her own hair. Twice a week she enjoyed an expensive treatment and blow-dry at the salon in town, but if she got it wet she had to blow-dry it herself and she had so much hair. So much thick, lustrous, glossy hair – the envy of many, of course – but which, in reality, was exhausting to style. However, today her mind was too busy for yoga. She knew that every pose she twisted herself into would be marred by anxiety that no amount of deep breathing could expel. Jasper was a grown man with

37

young children. He had to do *something*. He couldn't just waft about calling himself an entrepreneur when the good people of Badley Compton would expect so much more from Kenneth Scott-Booth's son. As her busy mind grew busier still, she slipped out of her dressing gown and dived into the water.

Later, after reading the *Daily Mail* and discarding it before Kenneth appeared for breakfast, Flappy sat at the island in the kitchen with an espresso and a bowl of fruit and glanced over the front page of *The Times*. Her eyes took in none of the words. If Flappy was good at one thing, it was knowing how to redirect negative energy into positive action. She would not let her anxieties overwhelm her. She would not be defeated – nor would she allow her indolent son to tarnish her reputation in this town. With a sudden rush of enthusiasm, she realized there was only one thing to do and one person capable of doing it. Flappy would have to find Jasper a job.

Kenneth appeared at nine in a pair of pink-and-green Pargyle trousers and a matching green golfing shirt. Flappy's jaw dropped. 'Good Lord, darling, where did those trousers come from?' She stared, horrified, at the garish sight.

'They're new in the shop,' he replied, striking a pose. Kenneth was clearly very pleased with his purchase. 'Dashing, don't you think?' he said. Flappy knew exactly which shop he was referring to, because the only shop he ever went into was the one at the golf club. Well, if those were the kind of things they were selling now they really ought to sack the buyer, she thought to herself. However, she did not want to upset her husband who obviously liked himself in them very much.

'Harlequin springs to mind,' she said drily.

'Jolly good,' he replied, pulling out a chair and sitting down. Flappy had already laid his place, as she did every morning. 'Harlequin's not a bad chap.'

'Though perhaps the matching shirt is a bit much,' she added tactfully. 'White might tone it down a bit, if you're happy to be toned down.'

Kenneth had never understood the words 'toned down' and he wasn't going to start now. When it came to golf, only the brightest and happiest colours would do. 'I copied the model in the window,' he explained. 'Didn't want to get it wrong.'

Flappy sniffed her disapproval, but this was not a battle worth fighting. 'Jasper will need a job,' she said, bringing over his cup of coffee and placing it on the table in front of him. 'He needs to do something, Kenneth. He can't float about living off his parents.'

Kenneth took a sip of coffee and made a grunting noise.

Flappy continued. 'It's all very well being generous, and you are, darling, enormously generous, but if you take away the incentive he'll never find his way in life. He'll just waft, and wafting is very undignified in a man of his age.'

Kenneth nodded. 'Quite right, Flappy. I'm sure he has something in mind.'

'Are you?' she replied, surprised. 'I'm afraid I don't share your optimism.'

'You underestimate him, darling. Let's wait until he's

settled in and then see. I can always find him a job at the golf course.'

'The golf course?' Flappy exclaimed hotly. 'Doing what, exactly? Being a caddy? Working in the shop selling Harlequin trousers? Waiting tables in the restaurant? He certainly can't sweep in and take over the place. What would people think? One simply can't behave like that these days. Nepotism is a definite no-no.' She brought Kenneth two slices of toast and sat down. 'No, Kenneth. He has to get a proper job. It's about time, don't you think? And I don't mean start up a cupcake business, or another bespoke gifting business, or open a coffee shop – goodness, there are enough of those sprouting up all over the place. I mean something proper.'

'I wonder what his game is like these days?' said Kenneth thoughtfully, buttering his toast and spreading a thick layer of strawberry jam on top.

Flappy sighed. There was nothing more to be said. 'I'm going to go and do my hair,' she told him, making for the door.

Kenneth turned his attention to *The Times*. 'Yes, Jasper's always had a good swing,' he muttered. 'It'll be good to have him on the golf course.'

As Flappy dried her hair in front of the mirror at her dressing table, her mind drifted to the Prices. After their collision in church on Sunday, she no longer felt like offering them her gardeners to plant a Himalayan rose underneath the apple tree in their garden. She *had* intended to make the gesture, she *had* fully intended to be generous, but now the wind had been taken out of her sails. She had lost the will. It wasn't like Flappy to be mean-spirited, but how could she possibly be otherwise when Molly Price had behaved in such a manner as to make benevolence impossible? How on earth was she going to get through dinner tonight? Being such an authentic person, Flappy found it hard to pretend, but pretend she would have to do, because it was beneath her dignity to be unfriendly. As queen of Badley Compton she knew very well that she must lead by example. It was what everyone expected of her. She must be gracious in the face of animosity, charming in the face of coarseness. Above all, she must show how very good she was at rising above the petty rivalries and ambitions of lesser folk.

When her hair was finished and, she had to admit, almost as beautifully coiffed as when she'd been to the salon, she turned her busy mind to her wardrobe. What was she going to wear tonight? Something casually elegant, perhaps. Something that showed off her figure and her style but did not give away the time and effort that had gone into putting the look together. 'Persephone!' she shouted down the stairs. Within seconds Persephone was hurrying up, her expression alert and expectant, ready to assist in that wonderfully enthusiastic way of hers that Flappy so admired. 'I need your advice. I have put together three outfits and I need you to tell me which I should wear tonight.'

Persephone laid her notebook down on the bed and went to the wardrobe where three ensembles were hanging on hangers hooked over the top of the door. She gave them a great deal of thought. Flappy approved of that. This was not a decision to be made lightly. This was dinner with the Prices and Flappy had to make the right impression.

'Well, the aquamarine necklace will enhance the colour of your eyes,' said Persephone thoughtfully. 'Trousers are casual smart but the Chanel jacket gives it that air of sophistication and urban chic. It shows that, although you live in Devon, you are someone not unfamiliar with London or Paris or Milan. But then, this powder-blue dress is effortlessly glamorous and feminine. Very Julia Roberts in *Pretty Woman*, although hers was brown. And, it's still warm. We're not really into autumn proper yet. You can get away with a summer dress, especially if you wear it with this lovely cashmere cardigan. The message here is that you are incredibly stylish without ever having to make the effort to be so. And finally, a long skirt and blouse, although it's pretty, I don't think it's right for tonight. It's a little mumsy, if you don't mind me saying. You don't want to look mumsy in front of the Prices.'

'Or ever,' Flappy added firmly.

Persephone smiled. 'I'm sure you wouldn't look mumsy. Only it appears a little frumpy on the hanger.'

'I'm going to go for the dress,' said Flappy. 'Thank you, Persephone.'

'Pleasure.'

'How's that man of yours?' she asked, referring to Hedda and Charles's son George.

Persephone beamed. 'He's lovely,' she replied. 'At the

moment we're spending weekends together. He comes here or I go up to London. We're planning a weekend in Paris.'

'How romantic.'

'Perhaps in October.'

'I do envy you, Persephone. All those romantic city breaks and holidays in the Caribbean ...' *And endless nights making love,* Flappy added silently, to herself. 'Those first few years of a relationship are precious. Enjoy them.'

'Oh, I intend to, Flappy,' said Persephone.

'They go so fast and then, suddenly, one realizes that one's home alone while one's husband is on the golf course in a hideous pair of Harlequin trousers, with a group of boring old men who can only talk about their swing and their handicap.' Flappy smiled with resignation. 'Well, I'm sure that's not *your* vision of the future, Persephone. George doesn't look like the sort of man who'd rather play sport than spend time with you.'

'It's early days,' she replied.

'It is, indeed. If golf rears its ugly head, nip it in the bud! That was my mistake. I was much too generous and kind at the beginning of our marriage. I should, perhaps, have been more demanding. But it's just not in my nature to be needy, and Kenneth so loves his golf.' Flappy shrugged. 'One can never find someone who ticks every box. The secret is to find someone who ticks the most important boxes. In that respect, I cannot complain about Kenneth.'

'If playing golf is his only fault, Flappy, I'd say you've done very well.'

Flappy narrowed her eyes. 'Well, it's not his *only* fault.

Kenneth is far from perfect. But, who am I to throw stones from my glass house.'

'I'd say you're pretty perfect, Flappy,' said Persephone.

Flappy grinned. 'That's why I hired you!'

In spite of her undisputed elegance and the shot of rum she'd tossed back before leaving the house, it was with a growing sense of unease that Flappy arrived at Compton Court with Kenneth, in the Jaguar, on the dot of eight. To her relief the Prices had not yet appeared, for the only cars parked on the forecourt were Hedda's navy-blue Mini Cooper and Charles's Bentley. She would have time, at least, for a glass of wine and a chat with Hedda before having to deal with Molly. Kenneth, in a pair of red chinos and an open-neck blue shirt and natural-coloured jacket she'd bought him in Hackett's, gave her a reassuring smile as they climbed the few steps up to the front door. He knew very well what Flappy thought of the Prices and he hoped, or rather he prayed, for the Prices' sake, that Molly would do nothing to further antagonize her. An antagonized Flappy was not a pleasant thing to behold. As much as she took pride in being able to dissemble with a gracious smile, there had been times when that veneer had slipped and an entirely alternative Flappy had seeped out with all the venom of a poisonous snake. He did not wish that on anyone, even the Prices who had, as Flappy put it, 'overstepped the mark'.

They had barely knocked when the big door opened and Johnson appeared, dapper in a black tailcoat, grey waistcoat and black tie, looking as if he'd come straight out of the International Butler Academy. Flappy was much too distracted to wish that she had such an elegant-looking butler at Darnley and followed him silently through the house to the drawing room where, to her surprise, Hedda and Charles were sitting talking to the Prices. Flappy was confounded. 'I thought we were the first,' she said, before even greeting them.

Molly smiled, the sweet smile of a woman in total ignorance of any faux pas she might have made. 'We never drive to dinner because we both like to drink, and we had to settle the children upstairs.' She held up her glass. 'What a treat. This is delicious. Gavi. My favourite.'

'*Che bello*,' said Flappy. '*Anch'io mi piace*.' And having shown off her perfect Italian, and seen the look of surprise and admiration on Molly Price's face, she began to feel a teeny bit better about the evening.

Chapter 4

Molly and Jim had not dressed up. As far as Flappy could see, neither had made the slightest effort. Molly was clearly a bohemian, in a long floral dress, leather ankle boots and a cardigan made out of crocheted squares sewn together to make a colourful patchwork. Jim was in a pair of black jeans, a grey shirt and a V-neck sweater that defied description on account of it being so bland. With his glasses, bald head and stubble, he looked *fashionable*. In fact, they both looked *fashionable*. Flappy gave a sniff, but she shook their hands and greeted them politely as if she were very pleased to see them.

How out of place they looked there, she thought, in Hedda and Charles's drawing room.

Flappy hoped no one noticed the lingering kiss Charles planted on her cheek. But in that moment, when his lips brushed her skin and his breath tickled her neck and the smell of him, the intoxicating smell of him that took her straight back to the bedroom in the cottage on those balmy late summer afternoons of uncontrolled passion, engulfed her senses, the rest of the room paled into insignificance. Flappy caught her breath and wished they were alone so that she could offer him her lips and allow him to kiss her deeply. 'You look ravishing,' he breathed and Flappy smiled and withdrew, knowing that a second longer with his hand on her waist and she'd give herself away most dreadfully.

Johnson brought Flappy and Kenneth glasses of wine on a silver tray and Flappy took a sip. The Gavi really was very good, she thought, taking another sip. Cold and crisp and just what she needed to get through the evening, which was going to be trying, for sure. Not only was Charles making her feel horribly uncertain, but Jim and Molly Price were just the sort of people to sorely try one.

Johnson disappeared, reappearing a moment later with the vicar and his wife, Graham and Joan Willis. Everyone stood up to greet them and any tension in the room was at once diffused by Graham's gentle charm and aura of holiness. Flappy responded to this aura of holiness by affecting an air of piety in order to impress the vicar and, by extension, God, with whom she had recently fallen a teeny bit into arrears. She spoke in a quieter voice, listened more intently and generally behaved as if she were in church. If there was one person who possessed the power to bring Flappy to her senses, it was the vicar. Joan sat on the sofa and immediately vanished into the upholstery, being so very plain.

'Do tell,' said Flappy to Molly, mustering up some enthusiasm. 'How is it going in Hollyberry House? I always thought that house could be quite beautiful given the right people inhabiting it.'

'We've unpacked, haven't we, Jim, but we haven't done anything to it yet. I think it's important to live in a place for a while before you do it up.'

'Very wise,' said the vicar in his vicarish voice, which carried more gravitas than anyone else's.

'We've only recently moved in here too,' said Hedda, glancing at Charles who was talking golf to Kenneth. 'It's the best thing we ever did, moving out of London.'

Molly's eyes gleamed. Flappy noticed that they were a very unusual shade of green, like sage in sunlight, and framed by thick black lashes. She could not deny it, Molly Price was, while not being a great beauty, strikingly pretty. 'That's what *I* think,' Molly replied. 'Jim wasn't so enthusiastic, were you, Jim? He likes the city. But I thought it better for the children to live in the country. Badley Compton is lovely. I think we're going to be very happy here.'

Flappy glanced at Jim and wondered whether he had a voice. 'Did you have a garden in London?' she asked, directing her question at Jim.

'Only a small one,' Molly replied. 'Here we have an enormous garden.' It wasn't, to be fair, anything like the size of the gardens at Darnley Manor, but Flappy humoured her all the same.

'Yes, it's a lovely garden,' she said, picturing it through a pair of binoculars. 'What are you going to do with that dead apple tree?'

Molly didn't appear at all surprised that Flappy knew about

the apple tree. 'I don't know,' she replied vaguely. 'Cut it down, probably.'

'If I were you, and I do know one or two things about gardens, I'd grow a Himalayan climber up it. We have one at Darnley and it really is quite spectacular.'

Molly's eyes widened. 'That's a great idea, Flappy.'

Flappy was pleased. So pleased, in fact, that she suddenly felt generous again towards the Prices. 'If you like, I'll lend you one of my gardeners. They're frightfully busy, but I'm sure I can spare one for an hour or two. It does make a difference having a professional opinion.'

Molly smiled and this time Flappy saw only gratitude in it. She wondered whether Molly's behaviour in church had simply been a misunderstanding. 'That's so kind of you. Thank you. I'd love to take you up on that offer. We don't have money to spend on a gardener and I know nothing about plants.'

Flappy raised her hand, her perfectly manicured hand, as if to say that thanks were not due. 'It's a pleasure, Molly. It's the least Kenneth and I can do to welcome you both to Badley Compton.'

'Yes,' Hedda echoed. 'We do want to welcome you to Badley Compton. When I arrived, everyone was so kind and welcomed me so warmly, Flappy and Kenneth especially. It's a rather unusual community in that way. Slightly old-fashioned. I suppose you could call it provincial, but I like to think Badley Compton is more sophisticated than that.'

'We don't want sophistication,' said Molly. 'Jim and I just

want peace.' She drained her glass and Flappy noticed a weary look pass over her face. Johnson appeared at once to pour more wine. Flappy also noticed a slight tremor in Molly's hand as she put the glass once more to her lips.

'What is it that you do, Molly?' asked Joan. Flappy and Hedda turned to the sofa in surprise.

'I used to be a columnist on *The Times*,' Molly replied, lowering her gaze. 'But now I'm trying something new.'

Joan raised her eyebrows, impressed. 'And Jim?' The women turned to Jim.

Molly was about to answer for him, when Flappy pre-empted her. 'Jim, I hear you're one of those brilliantly clever people who work with computers.'

Jim's expression barely changed. 'I'm a graphic designer,' he replied. Flappy tried to look interested, but it was hard. Computers, however creatively used, were even more boring than golf.

'Fascinating,' she said, squinting earnestly to show how very fascinated she was.

'The great thing is that we can both work from home,' said Molly quickly, and Flappy noticed that in the short time it had taken her to ask Jim what he did, Molly had quaffed her entire glass of wine. Flappy's eyes now narrowed with suspicion. If Flappy was good at one thing, it was reading between the lines when the lines themselves were quite misleading. She perceived that Molly was secretly resentful of Jim working from home. That Jim had not wanted to move out of London. That Molly had very likely been fired from her job at *The Times* and that, in all probability, she was teetering on the edge of alcoholism. For the first time since meeting her, Flappy felt sorry for Molly.

At dinner in Hedda's grand dining room, which, with its crimson walls and gilded picture frames, looked pleasingly aristocratic, Flappy was seated on Charles's left while Molly was placed on his right. On Flappy's other side was the vicar with Jim beside him. Poor Hedda had her work cut out. Flappy glanced over to see her chatting away with her usual ebullience while Jim ate his food in silence and looked bored. How very rude, Flappy thought. It was a definite no-no not to make an effort with the hostess.

It wasn't long before Flappy felt Charles's foot nudge hers beneath the table. At first it was simply a tap and could quite easily have been unintentional, but when it became more insistent, running up and down her ankle, Flappy was left in no doubt that Charles was playing a tacit game of footsie-footsie. She pulled her leg away and concentrated even more intently on what the vicar was saying. It had been years since anyone had toyed with Flappy's foot beneath a table. She had to admit, albeit with some reserve because Kenneth was only three places away, that she quite enjoyed the feeling. It was naughty. Forbidden. Daring. She took a large gulp of water – one glass of wine was enough for Flappy, who thought tipsiness exceedingly undignified – and straightened her back. Charles was playing a dangerous game. She couldn't allow it. She *mustn't* allow it. She looked at Hedda, her *dear* friend Hedda, who had been so big-hearted and generous when Flappy had confessed her brief affair with Charles, and thought that she'd rather die than let her down. No, she decided resolutely, she would not allow the temptations of the body to cloud the prudence of the mind. There had been many times in her life when she had had to draw upon *all* her reserves in order to do what was right. Now was one of those moments. 'Remind me, Graham, of the deeper significance of the Prodigal Son,' she asked.

At the end of dinner Hedda suggested the women accompany her to the drawing room for coffee. 'That's very old-fashioned,' said Molly with a giggle. She'd now had far too much to drink, Flappy noticed.

'Charles likes to smoke cigars,' said Hedda. 'Much better to leave the boys to drink their port in a fog of smoke, don't you think?'

Flappy, who, more than anyone, delighted in those out-dated aristocratic traditions, got up from her chair. 'It's lovely when things are done properly,' she said with approval.

Molly looked baffled. '*Is* it proper these days for women to leave the dining room so the men can discuss politics without offending our sensitive feminine ears?' She pulled a face to show how ridiculous she considered it to be.

Good Lord, thought Flappy in horror, *she's one of those militant feminists one reads about in the press.*

Hedda's smile did not waver. 'We in Badley Compton might seem rather provincial and old-fashioned to you modern young people, but it's traditions that keep our community together and in harmony. Take church, for example.' She paused. Flappy's eyes widened. If Hedda was going to scold her for taking her and Kenneth's seats, she was mightily impressed. 'You see, we all have our place and we all know where we stand,' she went on. 'Kenneth and Flappy have sat in the front pew for thirty years.'

'And Sir Algernon and Lady Micklethwaite lived here at Compton Court before moving to Spain,' Flappy cut in helpfully. 'They always sat in the front pew on the other side of the aisle, therefore, when Hedda and Charles moved in, the pew was rightfully passed on to them. You see, there's a structure, a system, an order. I wasn't going to say anything, because I was delighted that you and Jim, having only just moved here, should enjoy the view from the front row. From *our* front row. What sort of person would I be if I minded?' She gave a little sniff and a chuckle. 'But, when all is said and done, they are *our* seats. There are plenty of seats at the back of the church for newcomers.'

Charles and Kenneth were already lighting cigars and pouring the port. Graham, who didn't smoke, was sitting back in his chair with a benevolent look on his face. Jim had taken out his phone and was scrolling through his messages. Molly blinked at Flappy in amazement. 'God, I'm so sorry,' she gasped, looking very sorry indeed. 'I had no idea there was a . . .' She searched for the word.

Flappy leapt in to help her. 'Hierarchy?'

'Well, yes. I had no idea.' She put a hand on her heart. 'I really am very sorry.'

Flappy now felt even more kindly towards Molly, who seemed genuinely appalled and apologetic. She smiled sweetly. She had won the battle; now it was time to be mag-nanimous. 'Think nothing of it,' she said, glancing at the vicar and hoping he was witnessing her benevolence. 'It's a silly misunderstanding. I mean, how could you possibly have known?'

Hedda led the women back to the drawing room. Flappy was feeling triumphant but also compassionate. As much as Flappy liked to be on top, it gave her no pleasure to put other people down. Especially people like Molly Price who, she was beginning to realize, was an unhappy soul. Flappy, who, it was fair to say, was one of those rare *happy* souls, felt it her duty, being so very blessed, to nurture where nurturing was required. 'Molly,' she said, putting a gentle hand on the young woman's arm. 'I'm going to send my most experienced gardener to Hollyberry House tomorrow morning to advise you on how to make the best of your garden. And,' she added, pausing a second and crinkling her nose to show that now she was going to be even *more* generous, 'you are welcome to come to Darnley any time you like to see our gardens and how magnificent they look when things are done properly.'

It wasn't until the Prices and Willises had departed that Kenneth and Flappy were persuaded to remain a little longer for a post-mortem. 'Well, I thought that went very well,' said Kenneth, who, unlike his wife, had no sensitivity to the subtleties that lay between the lines.

'I'm sorry, darling, but I don't agree with you,' said Flappy. 'I thought Jim was extremely rude.'

'I agree with Flappy,' said Hedda. 'It was quite hard getting anything out of him during dinner. I was chattering away like a performing monkey and he was no help at all.'

'*She's* lively, though, and pretty,' said Charles, who was as inept at perceiving the undercurrents that flowed beneath the surface of things as Kenneth. 'Intelligent too. She knew a lot about art.'

Flappy bristled with jealousy. 'She might know a thing or two about art,' she said doubtfully, being herself a bit of an expert on the Italian Renaissance and the Impressionists. 'The truth is I don't think they're very happy. I think she's dragged him down here and he's wishing he was back in Bloomsbury.'

'He doesn't play golf,' said Kenneth, glancing at Charles and arching an eyebrow. 'I asked him.'

Hedda laughed. 'Oh, Kenneth, you *are* funny. Only *you* would ask a man who looks like he spends his entire life in a basement in front of a screen if he plays golf!'

Flappy laughed too. It was good to share a laugh with Hedda. 'Oh dear, they really are ill suited to the countryside, aren't they?'

'He told me he's going to build a gym,' said Charles. 'He likes to lift weights.'

'Really?' said Flappy. Jim didn't look capable of lifting much more than a knife and fork, she thought, but she didn't say it out loud. If there was one thing Flappy abhorred, it was criticizing the way people looked. After all, the poor man couldn't help being made the unfortunate way that he was. 'Well, working out is good for the mind,' she said. 'But what they really need to do is spend a little time in nature. Potter about the garden, go on lovely walks on the beach, let the fresh air blow London out of their hair.'

'He doesn't have any,' said Hedda, laughing again. She put a hand to her mouth. 'I'm sorry.' She tried to stop laughing but found she was unable to. 'I'm just so relieved they've gone. It was a dreadful, stodgy evening, let's be honest. But Molly got the message about church, which was the point of it.'

'You were very brave, Hedda,' said Flappy gratefully.

'And you and Kenneth are so good to have come and endured this ghastly evening. Thank you, both. I don't know what I'd do without you.'

And Flappy was happy she was able to return the compliment, genuinely, from the heart. 'We're just so *so* lucky to have friends like you,' she said.

Flappy sat in the passenger seat of Kenneth's Jaguar and opened her evening bag in search of her lip gloss. What she found was a piece of white paper, folded neatly and slipped into the inside pocket. Her heart stalled. She glanced at Kenneth, who was busy looking at the road ahead as he motored towards home. Flappy knew she couldn't read it in front of him.

As soon as she was in her bedroom, she opened the note. A blush lit up her cheeks and spread down to her chest. *These are the things I want to do to you . . .* Charles had written. Then he had listed them. Flappy feasted her eyes upon the brief descriptions and felt her blood grow hot. *How daring of him,* she thought with a shiver of excitement. She sank onto the bed with a sigh of longing and regret. Allowing her gaze to settle unfocused in the half-distance, she permitted herself to remember Charles's touch. If only she hadn't promised Hedda ... But she *had*, and a promise made was a promise kept. Flappy was unwavering about that.

She took a deep breath, shook Charles out of her mind and tore the note into tiny pieces.

The next morning Flappy was true to her word, as Flappy always was, and sent her head gardener, Andy Pritchett, round to the Prices'. Satisfied that her gesture would be well received and once again feeling a wave of compassion for poor unhappy Molly, she set about doing all the important things she had to do on a Thursday morning. Persephone was busy at her desk, on the telephone mostly, getting quotes for Flappy's *ballo in maschera,* and Kenneth had departed for the golf course. Flappy sat at her own desk in her study, a charming and serene room decorated in soft greens and pinks that looked out over the lawn, one of the *various* lawns they had at Darnley, and put on her reading glasses. She had letters to read and a vast number of things to arrange because the Harvest Festival tea was approaching and not long after that, the Halloween fancy dress children's parade, all hosted by Flappy herself here at Darnley. Among those events were various committee meetings and book club meetings, all of which depended on Flappy for direction and leadership. She sighed beneath the weight of so much responsibility, but if Flappy was good at one thing, it was putting civic duty above her own pleasure. Really, what sort of person would she be if she spent her days drifting around her magnificent gardens, enjoying her beautiful house and ignoring the needs of the lesser folk in town?

At the end of the afternoon, when she finally put her feet up – well, not *literally*, Flappy disapproved of people who put their shoes on the furniture – there was a knock at the drawing-room door and Andy Pritchett hovered there, looking a little embarrassed to be bothering her.

'Hello, Andy,' said Flappy, putting down her teacup.

'Sorry to interrupt, Mrs Scott-Booth,' he said, removing his cap. Andy Pritchett was a robust fifty-year-old with greying hair and a wide, handsome face, weathered to a nut brown by years of working outside. 'Mrs Price has asked whether she might borrow me tomorrow.'

Flappy frowned. She'd been quite happy to lend him for a day, but two was surely taking advantage of her good nature. 'I see,' she said.

'She likes the idea of a Himalayan rose climbing up her apple tree and has asked whether I might plant one.'

'I don't suppose you can buy one at the garden centre, can you?'

'I'll have to order it.'

'And then return to plant it, I assume?'

'Yes.'

Flappy picked up her teacup. She did have a whole team of gardeners, she conceded. It wouldn't hurt to lend Andy for another day, and poor Molly Price needed all the help she could get. 'Her garden's in a dreadful state, isn't it?' she said.

'I'm afraid it needs a lot of work.'

'Yes, I imagine it does. Well, the gardens here at Darnley can survive another day without you, I suppose.'

'Thank you,' he said. 'Mrs Price will be very pleased. I think she's a little overwhelmed.'

'No good deed goes unpunished,' she added with a sigh. 'Tell me, Andy, are they settling in?'

'I haven't seen Mr Price, only Mrs. She seems a bit on edge.'

Flappy narrowed her eyes. 'Yes, I thought she seemed a little on edge last night at dinner. I'm sure they'll find their feet. It's not easy, I imagine, moving from the city to a town like Badley Compton. It's probably too quiet for them.'

'She told me the quiet is what they need,' said Andy.

Flappy raised an eyebrow. 'Let's hope they find it then,' she replied.

Later that evening Flappy trod lightly over the lawn to the pretty white cottage with the thatched roof that sat in the cosy embrace of a horse chestnut tree at the bottom of the garden. It had once been her painting studio, but she realized, having painted enough *grands oeuvres* to adorn the walls of the great and good of Badley Compton, that she really didn't have time to spend hours at her easel, and it would serve her better as a sanctuary, a place where she could come and meditate in front of her Buddha shrine for an hour or so in the evenings. A place she could be alone.

Once a week she invited the ladies, Mabel, Madge, Esther and Sally, to do yoga with her and meditate under the guidance of Murli, her guru. Murli was a proper guru from Rajasthan, an enlightened man sent by the Universe to help Flappy advance up the path towards her own Enlightenment. The ladies, it must be said, lagged a teeny bit behind her on that path, but being the generous soul that she was, Flappy felt it her duty to carry them with her – and it did give her the opportunity to show how very flexible she was in the limbs and how deeply she could go when communing with her Higher Self in meditation. The Universe had been generous enough to send her a guru when she'd put out the word that she wanted one; it was the least she could do to share him.

Now, however, Flappy was alone. She opened the door to the cottage and stepped inside, inhaling with satisfaction the scent of incense (the very same incense used in Buddhist temples) and settling her eyes onto the jade Buddha her decorator Gerald had acquired from Vietnam. Well, to be honest, he'd bought it in a shop in Chestminster, but it had been imported from Vietnam, which made it authentic. Flappy was all for cutting corners when corners needed to be cut.

Her eyes strayed up the stairs and she was assaulted by a sudden pang of longing. Oh, for those afternoons making love with Charles in the big bed up there under the eaves. How delicious they had been. How wicked. But she didn't allow herself to dwell on something lost, and instead sat cross-legged on the carpet in front of the shrine and closed her eyes. As she began to chant 'Om', the image that surfaced in her mind of Charles, so handsome and forbidden, was replaced by Jasper and Briony and their imminent arrival in Badley Compton. She tried to turn their faces into clouds, but they were big, black, solid clouds that wouldn't blow away. Clouds full of stress and anxiety which, however much she tried to align herself with the vibration of the Universe, rained upon her with all their incumbent inconveniences.

Chapter 5

On Friday morning Flappy received a text that read, simply: *Landed*. Flappy pursed her lips. How very typical of Jasper to be so brief, she thought, a trifle peeved. He was more poetic when in need of money. She switched off her telephone and headed into town in her Range Rover, listening to Olly Murs singing 'Please Don't Let Me Go' on Radio 1; it was, after all, important to know what the young were listening to. She parked the car at the kerb and walked down the high street to Big Mary's Café Délice. Inside, at a round table by the window, Mabel and the ladies were waiting for her. At the sight of Flappy, so incongruous in her elegant trousers, tailored jacket and gold jewellery, the quartet sat up sharply. Flappy was on time; they had arrived fifteen minutes early.

Flappy sat down and pushed her oversized sunglasses onto the top of her head. 'Isn't this nice!' she exclaimed. 'Meeting like this. To think I rarely set foot in here. I've been missing all the fun. What are you having?' She glanced at their plates. By the look of the crumbs it would have been more appropriate to have used the past tense.

'Shall I get you a cup of coffee?' asked Mabel, standing up.

'Oh, would you? Thank you.'

'I don't suppose you want anything else. A cake? A bun?' she said, then added, because she knew how much Flappy liked France, 'A croissant?'

'Oh, all right, if you insist. I'll have a slice of chocolate cake.' Flappy smiled at the others. 'It would be churlish of me to put the preservation of my figure above mucking in with you.' The truth was that today of all days Flappy was in dire need of cake.

'Today's the day,' said Sally, grinning at Flappy.

'For what?' said Flappy, looking bewildered.

'Jasper's arriving in Badley Compton,' said Sally.

'You must be beside yourself with excitement,' said Madge.

'Yes, *very* excited,' said Flappy, trying to inject some excitement into her voice.

'I hear they're renting that pretty house next to the pub,' said Esther. Flappy's smile did not waver, but that was the first she'd heard of it. Jasper had been typically economical with the details. She wondered how Esther knew about it when she did not.

'How lovely,' Madge gushed. 'It's one of the prettiest houses in town.'

'The landlord, Gus Trent, rides my horses twice a week and told me all about it,' said Esther.

'I'm glad to see the Badley Compton grapevine is in good working order,' said Flappy. 'Yes, he and Briony are moving into that charming house. At least he won't have to go very far to get a drink in the evenings.' She laughed, but it grated that Esther knew more about Jasper's plans than she did.

Mabel returned with Flappy's cup of coffee and cake. 'Isn't it exciting!' she gushed. 'Jasper arriving today, all the way from Australia. When does he fly in? I can't wait to see him and to meet his wife and children. The last time I saw Jasper was when he'd graduated from Cambridge and was setting off to start working on the other side of the world. Do you remember, Flappy? Is he still as handsome as he was then? So like you. Lovely that your good looks passed on to your children. Would have been such a shame if they hadn't.'

Flappy took a bite of cake. The sugar rush made her feel instantly better. 'I'm not one to boast about my children, as you know,' she said when her mouth was empty – it was very undignified to speak with one's mouth full. 'So I can't comment on whether or not he's still handsome and besides, I'm biased. But I do remember that moment, Mabel. His future was so golden. So full of promise.' She sighed, masking, as only Flappy could, the truth, which was not quite so golden or promising. 'I am so *so* lucky that he and his charming wife Briony are coming to live here, in Badley Compton. I mean, they could have chosen anywhere in England, anywhere at all, but they chose here, near me and Kenneth. Such a compliment and one I'm sure I don't deserve. I've been a useless grandmother. I barely know my grandchildren.'

'But now you'll have the opportunity to get to know them,' said Sally.

'They probably chose Badley Compton for the free babysitting service,' said Esther with a chuckle.

Flappy did *not* see herself babysitting. In fact, the image of those small children putting grubby fingers on her upholstery and dropping food onto her immaculate carpets filled her with horror. 'Oh yes,' she exclaimed. 'I'll be on hand for that. I can't wait to be a useful grandmother.'

With that she popped the rest of the cake into her mouth and allowed the delicious taste of chocolate to suppress the bitter taste of trepidation.

Flappy drove home fighting an uneasy battle between maternal instinct and pride, which lamented the fact that Jasper was not the kind of son who covered her in his reflected glory. Jasper was not glorious. Certainly, he was handsome with a happy-go-lucky charm (easy to be happy-go-lucky when your father paid all the bills) but, floating around doing nothing, for a man with a family to feed, was a definite no-no. Why couldn't he stay in Australia and float about doing nothing there? Her misgivings were compounded by the thought of Jasper's competitive, pretentious wife. Flappy was not looking forward to their arrival. If there was one thing she abhorred, it was competitive, pretentious people.

Therefore, it was with some reluctance that she had invited them all for dinner so that they wouldn't have to worry about food on their first evening in Badley Compton. Kenneth was understandably excited. He loved his son very much and thought the world of Briony. If he noticed that Flappy had reservations about her daughter-in-law, he never mentioned it. In Kenneth's world everything was harmonious and happy, like a day at the golf course.

Flappy had gone to great lengths to make the house look its best. She'd instructed Persephone to buy an enormous arrangement of lilies for the hall table. Karen, who often came to cook, had prepared a delicious dinner and lit all the scented candles in the dining room and drawing room. Flappy had asked Kenneth to play some soothing classical music and, in order to look *her* best (she didn't want to be outshone by her daughter-in-law), she'd had a blow-dry at the salon and fresh polish applied to her nails – a graceful shell-pink. She heard the scrunching of tyres on gravel at six-thirty. She swept down the stairs in a long pleated skirt and black sleeveless sweater, looking every inch a Ralph Lauren model.

Flappy opened the door to find Jasper and Briony, *sans* children, standing on the doorstep. 'Darling, how lovely you're here!' she exclaimed, drawing Jasper into a warm embrace. Seeing him in the flesh, with his winning smile and twinkling eyes full of humour and affection, dispelled some of the worry that had been plaguing her. He really was devilishly good-looking. She could be proud of *that*. 'And Briony, you must be exhausted and yet you look as fresh as a daisy.' Briony did, indeed, look immaculate. In indigo-coloured jeans and a nippy black jacket, her blonde hair falling in waves over her shoulders, she looked polished and expensive. The expensive bit of her look did, however, grate on Flappy's good nature. Nonetheless, she kissed Briony on her frosty cheek. Two chiselled bones clashing as their faces came together. 'But where are the children?'

'At home.' Briony turned to Jasper and smiled. 'I do love to say that. *Home.*' Turning back to Flappy, she added, 'With the au pair.'

'You have an au pair?' asked Flappy in surprise.

'We brought her with us,' Jasper told her, striding into the house to embrace his father. *Well,* Flappy thought, *that's clearly what he needed the extra money for. Another plane ticket!*

Kenneth and Jasper hugged as men do, patting each other on the back. Then Kenneth did the same to Briony but without the patting. Briony stiffened. Kenneth, of course, didn't notice and pressed his big belly against her flat one with enthusiasm. 'You must both be in need of a drink,' he said. 'Let's go into the drawing room.'

Kenneth walked ahead with Jasper while Briony followed behind with Flappy. 'You have a beautiful house, Flappy,' she said, then her eyes rested on the portraits of Kenneth and Flappy that dominated the wall. 'Are those by Jonathan Yeo?' she asked.

Flappy smiled, pleased that she'd noticed them. They were very fine, especially the one of her. Charles had called it 'a masterpiece'. 'Yes, they're rather good, aren't they?'

'They're *really* good,' said Briony. Flappy tried not to be irritated by Briony's Australian accent. Perhaps now living in England she would lose it and speak proper English, like Flappy did. 'Maybe we'll get our portraits done when we buy our own house,' she said.

Flappy made no comment. She knew very well that Jasper did not have the money to purchase a property and she was damned if Kenneth was going to buy one for them. Instead, she moved towards the drawing room and asked Briony about her flight. 'It's just bearable in business,' Briony replied, without any hint of gratitude. 'At least we could bed down and get some sleep. I think the kids watched movies and played games for most of the journey.'

If there was one thing Flappy abhorred, it was the word 'kids'. It was a horror. Above all, it was common. Flappy put a hand on Briony's arm and patted it in a motherly kind of way. 'One doesn't say "kids" at Darnley,' she said, crinkling her nose and smiling generously to show that it was not meant unkindly. 'One says "children". I do think "kids" strips them of their dignity, don't you?'

Briony laughed. She tossed her long, wavy blonde hair and smiled her big, toothy smile. 'Oh, Flappy!' she cried. 'You really are wonderful.'

Flappy looked puzzled. 'I don't think I am,' she said. 'Language is important.'

Briony took the glass of wine that Kenneth offered her. 'Well, it'll be "children" from now on,' she said. 'And, if there are any other words you'd prefer me not to use at Darnley, do let me know. I don't want to get it wrong.'

Flappy wasn't sure whether Briony was mocking her or being agreeable, which for Flappy was an uncomfortable position to be in. Above all, she liked to have the upper hand. 'Let's sit down, shall we?' she said, sinking into the sofa and feeling strangely at a disadvantage.

Briony sat beside Jasper on the sofa opposite and Flappy noticed her hand settle onto his knee, where it remained, as if staking a claim. 'It's so great to be here,' she said. 'There's something so exciting about starting over in a new place.' Flappy thought of Molly Price. The two women shared the same enthusiasm for moving to Badley Compton.

'The house is to your liking?' asked Kenneth, perching on the club fender with his knees wide to make space for his belly.

'It's perfect,' said Jasper, who had his father's positivity.

Briony, however, did not. 'I wouldn't call it a house. It's a cottage, really. It's a little small,' she said, crinkling her nose in the way Flappy did when she wanted to sugar-coat a criticism. 'I mean, it's fine. I'm not complaining. But with two boisterous kids, I mean *children*, there's not a lot of room for them to run around in.'

'But you have the great outdoors,' said Flappy. 'And a garden? You do have a garden, don't you?'

'We have a lovely garden,' said Jasper.

'Well, that's a little small too. But it's fine. It'll do, until—'

Flappy did not want Briony mentioning buying a house in front of Kenneth. 'You must come and use our pool,' she cut in. 'That'll entertain the children, and they're welcome, of course, to tear about our gardens.' She regretted the offer just as she said it, and the image of the children trampling through the herbaceous border and picking the heads off flowers caused her stomach to clench with panic. Tom and Jack, if she remembered rightly from last year's Christmas holiday in the Caribbean, were seven and five and indeed very boisterous. She would instruct one of the gardeners to keep an eye on them, she decided, and the panic in her stomach subsided somewhat.

'We'd love to use the pool,' said Briony. 'I'm a real water baby and so are the boys.'

'Good,' said Kenneth. 'I'll take them to the putting range. How's your game, Jasper?'

'Not bad, Dad.'

'Fancy one tomorrow?'

'Won't you be unpacking?' said Flappy.

'We've put most of our stuff into storage,' said Jasper. He looked fondly at his wife. 'And Briony likes to unpack and put everything away neatly, don't you, darling? I might as well get out of the house and leave her to it.'

'Jasper's right. I'm a bit OCD. I like everything to be just so. Flappy, you're going to have to show me around the town. I need to know where to get flowers and if there's a nice deli – I definitely need to know where that is. I like everything to be organic and of the very best quality.'

'Are you still vegetarian?' asked Flappy, hoping that she wasn't, for Karen had cooked a lamb tagine.

'I was right up until recently, but I read a very interesting article claiming it's detrimental to one's health not to eat meat. We are, after all, meat-eating creatures.'

'It was another fad,' said Jasper, shaking his head and laughing. 'Briony is always following one fad or another.'

'Oh, Jasper, that's not fair. Some people explore the world, I explore my *inner* world.'

'You sound like Flappy,' said Kenneth. 'If you're talking

meditation, you should see her sanctuary in the cottage.'

'A sanctuary?' Briony's pretty eyes lit up with interest.

'Oh, it's nothing,' said Flappy, waving her pale pink fingernails in the air, hoping to play it down. She didn't want those boisterous children in there, nor did she particularly want Briony.

'She even has a Buddha shrine,' Kenneth continued.

'I use it for quiet time, alone. No one else. Only me. Me and Buddha. One is so terrifically busy, it's important to check out every now and then.'

'And go within,' said Briony, giving her husband a knowing look. 'I've tried to convince Jasper to meditate but without success.'

'I can't close my eyes and do nothing,' he said. 'I either fall asleep or twitch with boredom.'

'Will you show me your sanctuary?' Briony asked Flappy. 'I'd love to have a quiet little place I can go and meditate in. Somewhere away from the boys and the general noise of life.'

Flappy's smile remained, although behind it she was seething with irritation that Kenneth could be so careless and mention her shrine. The last thing she needed was Briony taking it over – as well as her pool and gardens. She felt the clench of panic once again. 'Of course,' she said, but already her busy mind was frantically searching for a reason why she couldn't.

They were halfway through dinner when Flappy brought up the subject of work. 'What are you going to do here?' she asked Jasper. 'Have you any plans? Any ideas? Do share them. Your father and I would love to know.'

71

Jasper grinned at Kenneth. The charming, winning grin that had induced so many large cheques in the past and very likely would continue to induce them long into the future. 'Dad has been so generous,' he said and his aquamarine eyes, the same unusual shade as his mother's, misted. 'You know, I've really appreciated your help over the years. It hasn't been easy. I've had a bit of bad luck here and there.' Flappy wanted to say that one makes one's own luck, but she didn't want to interrupt Jasper's sweet speech, although, she suspected, it was a teeny bit cynical. 'I'm going to take my time settling in. As you know, we have our hearts set on staying here, permanently. It's where I grew up.' He turned to his mother, the same misty-eyed look, intending, Flappy knew, to bend her to his will. 'It's home. It's where I want to raise my own children. But regarding work, I have the odd idea, but nothing concrete. When I know for sure, I'll give you the big reveal.'

'My breath is bated,' said Flappy drily.

Kenneth wiped his mouth with a napkin. 'Delicious, Flappy,' he said.

'Yes, delicious, Mum. You're a great cook.'

'Oh, it's nothing. Just a simple tagine,' said Flappy, who was not going to admit that she hadn't cooked it.

Kenneth looked at his son and smiled. Flappy knew that smile. It was the same one he gave her when she asked for something big, like a new car, a villa in the Algarve or an extravagant, Italian-inspired masked ball. Kenneth never said no. 'We'll talk man to man, later,' he said with a wink. 'Right now, I want to toast your arrival in Badley Compton and to

72

say how happy your mother and I are that you've decided to come home. You know we'll always be here for you.'

Jasper's eyes misted further. They clinked glasses. 'Thanks, Dad. Thanks, Mum. Really, you're the best parents a boy could have.' And there was nothing Flappy could say to that.

The following morning, at nine, just as Flappy had sat down with Kenneth to keep him company while he ate his breakfast, she heard the doorbell. Flappy frowned. Who could be ringing their bell at nine o'clock on a Saturday morning? She put down her teacup and went into the hall. To her surprise, a young woman she didn't recognize stood on the doorstep with two small children in tow. Flappy recognized the children at once. Her grandchildren, Tom and Jack. 'Ah, you must be the au pair,' she said. Then it registered. They'd come for the pool.

'Yes, I'm Kim,' said the young woman. 'Mrs Scott-Booth told me to come and use your pool.'

Flappy was astonished how quickly Briony had taken her up on her offer. Still, the two expectant faces of her grandchildren, gazing up at her with a mixture of shyness and fear, softened the affront. 'Hello, Tom. Hello, Jack,' she said in her sweetest, most grandmotherly voice. 'How lovely to see you both. Come on in. I'll show you where everything is.'

The trio followed her into the hall. She showed them the kitchen for drinks and snacks and made a point of emphasizing the sink, for washing hands – she did not want jam on her cushions. Kenneth shook Kim's hand and ruffled the boys' hair and told them how much they had grown since he had last seen them. Then Flappy took them down to the pool, which was housed in an annex they had built when they'd moved in, with big glass doors, opening onto a wide terrace and a rose garden. Flappy was very proud of the pool house, being as it was so tastefully decorated in pale blues and greys. Her gaze strayed a moment to the changing rooms where Charles had taken her for the first time in a frenzy of uncontrollable passion and she felt a stab of longing. This was quickly suppressed for Flappy knew that now was not a moment for those kinds of recollections. She turned her attention once again to her grandsons.

The boys livened up when they laid their eager eyes on the water and the mosaic hippo who stared up at them from the bottom of the shallow end. They began running around the edge, pointing at it and laughing. Flappy noticed their Australian accents and hoped that, by attending an English school, they'd swiftly lose them. 'There are towels in the changing rooms,' she told Kim. 'If you need anything, give a shout. But I'm sure you'll find your way around.'

'Thank you very much, Mrs Scott-Booth,' said Kim. 'The kids are going to have a blast.'

'I'm sure they are,' Flappy agreed, ignoring her use of the word 'kids'. After all, Kim was the au pair; 'kids' was exactly the sort of word she'd expect her to say.

Flappy went back upstairs to find that Kenneth had finished his breakfast and left for the golf course. She'd intended to go into town, but now Kim had arrived with her grandsons she was reluctant to leave them alone in the house. There was no telling what they might get up to. She didn't want to return to find the house turned upside down, although, she had to concede, Kim did seem to be a responsible and well-mannered young woman.

Flappy wandered into the kitchen to make herself a cup of coffee when the telephone rang. She left it to ring the usual eight times before answering. 'Darnley Manor, Flappy Scott-Booth speaking.'

'Flappy, it's Mabel.'

'Hello, Mabel.'

'Are you busy?'

'When am I not terrifically busy? Right now I've got my grandsons here. They're having a lovely time in the pool. I must say, it's just heaven to watch them splashing about so happily.'

'How lovely that they're here,' Mabel gushed.

'I know, I'm so *so* lucky that they've chosen to live a stone's throw from Darnley. I must tell you, Jasper was very touching last night at dinner. He said it had always been his desire to come home. Well, there's no place like Darnley, is there?'

'No, there isn't,' Mabel agreed. 'I was just ringing to find out how it went last night. I've been thinking about you all morning. Are they happy with the house?'

'Very. It is a delightful house, after all. One of the most charming to be found in Badley Compton.'

'And next to the pub,' Mabel laughed. 'I bet Jasper's happy about that.'

Flappy laughed too. 'He won't have to worry about drink driving, will he. It's almost too convenient.'

'What's he going to do, workwise?'

Flappy didn't miss a beat. 'He's working on something very exciting but won't tell us what it is.'

'Ooooh! I love a secret. How gripping. I'm sure it's something wonderful. The apple doesn't fall far from the tree, does it?'

'No, it doesn't, although I doubt very much it's got anything to do with food.'

'He'll want to do something different to what his father did, won't he. I can't wait to hear what it is. I bet it's something very special. That Jasper is so enterprising.'

Flappy's heart sank. 'He is,' she lied. 'Very enterprising.' If there was one thing Flappy was good at, it was hiding her children's shortcomings when they needed to be hidden.

'And one more thing,' said Mabel.

'Yes?' Flappy replied.

'I spotted a long-tailed skua,' Mabel announced proudly. 'After you saw one last week, I made a point of looking it up in my bird directory and going out with my binoculars.'

'Really?' said Flappy, who wasn't even sure what a long-tailed skua looked like.

'Really,' Mabel repeated. 'You were so clever to spot it and I just got lucky, I suppose. Next time you go out with your binoculars, I'd love to come with you.'

'Of course,' said Flappy, but unless she needed to spy on the Prices again, her binoculars were going to remain safely in the drawer.

Chapter 6

The following morning Flappy and Kenneth went to church. No longer anxious that the Prices were going to sit in their seats, Flappy did, however, feel a teeny bit uneasy about where Jasper and Briony were going to sit. They had not intended to go, being jetlagged, but Flappy had insisted. They were, after all, members of the First Family of Badley Compton, if one could call the Scott-Booths by that title, which one could, Flappy thought reasonably. It was important that they do the right thing and join the community in their Sunday worship. They should really, by rights, sit in the same pew as her and Kenneth, but as the Prices had demonstrated the week before, there was simply no room due to the buttress shortening the row. Surely someone would move to accommodate them.

It came as some surprise then, when Flappy entered the church a few minutes before the service was due to start, to find Jasper, Briony, Tom and Jack sitting in the same back row as Molly and Jim and their children. Jasper gave his parents a smile and Briony waved discreetly, and no one seemed to mind that they were in such unimportant seats. In fact, they looked perfectly content there. As Flappy swept by she caught, out of the corner of her eye, Molly and Briony putting their heads together in a whispered conversation. Something about those two young women coming together gave Flappy an uneasy feeling. A feeling of impending doom.

Flappy and Kenneth took their seats in the front row. Flappy cast her gaze across the aisle and caught Charles's eye. He winked at her. A wink that held within it all the deliciously naughty things he had done to her in the cottage at the bottom of the garden. She returned his wink with a blush until Hedda looked her way and beamed a smile and then Flappy beamed one back and felt a little better about Charles's indecent wink. As long as Hedda stood between them she was safe, not only from Charles, but from herself. She turned her attention back to the vicar and called upon God to give her strength not to stray once again from His ways.

As the congregation knelt down to pray, Flappy wondered how she'd feel if Charles *stopped* winking at her. If he winked at Molly instead. If he treated her like everyone else and ceased telling her how beautiful she was and how in love with her he was. How would she feel then? The truth was – and there was no better time to be truthful than on one's knees in church – that she would mind very much. She liked to think that she was a woman of little pride and vanity, but Charles had inspired in her both those sinful qualities. The fact was that she *did,* indeed, feel proud that at her age she still appealed to a handsome man like Charles. Charles was like the devil tempting her to break God's Ten Commandments and making rather a good job of it.

Once the service was over and Kenneth had pushed a crisp note into the collection bag, Flappy filed out with Hedda, deliberately leaving Charles to walk behind with Kenneth – although she could feel Charles's eyes upon her back as if his gaze were made of laser beams. Once out in the damp grey churchyard, she noticed at once a small group of young people talking together at the bottom of the path: the Prices, Jasper and Briony and, most surprisingly of all, Persephone and George. They looked as if they were getting on extremely well. Briony was tossing back her blonde hair, Jasper was speaking, his handsome face aglow with humour and charm, George and Persephone were laughing and, to Flappy's astonishment, Jim was smiling. It wasn't the biggest smile, to be sure, but it was the most animated Flappy had seen him.

'Look at that!' she said to Hedda. 'Jim Price is coming out of his shell.'

'Birds of a feather,' Hedda replied. 'I suppose it was only a matter of time before that group found each other.' Hedda's expression softened. 'It's lovely having George home for the weekend. Persephone's a sweet girl. It's early days, but I have a very good feeling about those two.'

'I do too,' said Flappy. 'Although selfishly, I don't want her to leave Badley Compton and go and live with George in London. You know, she's not just my PA. She's like my daughter, but better. I can only say this to you, Hedda, but I've always had a bit of a strained relationship with my girls.'

'Families are often difficult, because you don't choose them like you choose your friends. Sometimes the personalities clash. It's normal.'

'You're so wise.'

'Seeing as we're being frank with each other,' said Hedda, leaning closer to Flappy and lowering her voice, 'George isn't really enjoying his job.'

Flappy's eyes widened with interest. 'Really?'

'He's unsatisfied.'

'Unsatisfied is an awful thing to be,' said Flappy. 'What's he going to do about it?'

'I don't know, but I'd like him to find something down here.'

'There must be an architect's firm in Chestminster he can work for.'

'I'm not sure that's what he wants to do anymore. Persephone has made him look at the world through different eyes.'

'Do you think he might be looking to move to Badley Compton?' Flappy held her breath.

'He hasn't said so, but *I* would like him to move here. That way I get my son and you get to keep Persephone.'

'Oh, Hedda, I can barely dare hope.'

'Don't breathe a word of this to anyone.'

'My lips are sealed.' And they truly were, because if Flappy was good at one thing, it was knowing when it was advantageous to keep a secret.

The following week was a busy one for Flappy. Persephone found a stunning Italianesque marquee for Flappy's *ballo in maschera* and booked a catering company to serve an Italian banquet. She had also managed to engage the services of a company in Chestminster who made theatre sets. They were confident they could transform the interior of the marquee into a vision of Venice, complete with bridges and gondolas. Flappy was delighted. Persephone had also mocked up an invitation, and a calligrapher was booked to write the names and addresses. Flappy spent most of the week writing and rewriting the guest list. Unlike Hedda for her party, she was *not* going to invite everyone. She was going to be more discerning. More selective. Ruthless.

Every evening, after school, Tom and Jack came to swim with Kim. Flappy showed Kim a side entrance so that she could let herself in without bothering her. Briony not only used the swimming pool herself, but Flappy's gym too and, to add insult to injury, reminded Flappy about showing her the cottage. Flappy promised her she would, when she wasn't so busy. 'This week is hectic, I'm afraid,' she told Briony. 'I haven't got a single moment to myself.' Which wasn't strictly true, but Flappy was damned if she was going to allow Briony to take over her sanctuary too.

By the end of the week, Jasper and Briony had settled into their house and bought a dog. Flappy did *not* like dogs, but before she knew it, the rescue retriever named Buster was charging about her gardens, the *many beautiful* gardens at Darnley, with the two boys running along behind without any consideration for the neatly maintained borders and flower beds. Even though it was autumn and the gardeners were cutting back shrubs and gathering leaves, Flappy did not want the dog and the children running wild and being a nuisance. However, when she tried to call them away from her prized herbaceous border, one of the gardening team popped his head out of a viburnum and said that they were no trouble at all. It was a joy to see the trio having so much fun. And Flappy did not want to be seen as a bad grandmother. 'I was only thinking about you being disturbed,' she replied. 'As long as you don't mind, I'll allow them to enjoy the space. I am, after all, so *so* lucky to have so much space here at Darnley, it's only fair that I share it.'

And share it she did. A lot.

Jasper played golf with Kenneth and then, in the evenings, played tennis with Charles, who, as well as being a superb golfer was also a superb tennis player. Flappy wondered whether her son was even thinking about getting a job or whether he was just going to be a man of leisure, skipping from the golf course to the tennis courts of Compton Court and Darnley Manor without a care in the world. She hadn't asked Kenneth but she suspected he had written out a large cheque during that man-to-man chat.

Jasper, Briony and the boys might not have shown any gratitude for Flappy's generosity in allowing them to come and go at Darnley as if they owned the place, but Kenneth did. Kenneth could always be relied upon to notice his wife's many acts of kindness and to comment upon them. 'You really are big-hearted, darling,' he said when they lay side by side in the master bed. 'That's one of the things I most like about you. You're always thinking of other people and never thinking about yourself.'

'Oh, that's so sweet of you to say, Toad,' Flappy replied, feeling affectionate suddenly in the warmth of his praise.

'I want to do something for *you* for a change. You do so much for me.'

'I don't need anything, darling,' said Flappy.

'How typical of you to be so unmaterialistic.'

'You're letting me throw a New Year's Eve ball, after all,' she added, aware that the *ballo in maschera* was going to cost him a fortune.

'But that's just another example of your munificence,' he said, his small eyes twinkling at her gratefully. 'You know how much I love a party.'

'It's true, I do,' Flappy conceded.

'I'm going to buy you a very special Christmas present,' he said. 'A surprise. I know how you love a surprise. As we're spending Christmas at Darnley this year, I can buy you something big.'

'Darling, it's not the size that counts but the thought behind it.'

'Big present, big thought. Leave it to me.' And with that he put his magazine on the bedside table and switched off the light.

Flappy had not given the Prices a thought since Sunday when she'd seen them again at church, sitting in the back row with Jasper, Briony and their children as they'd done the Sunday before. However, her sharp antennae were raised on the following Tuesday when Andy Pritchett asked whether Mrs Price could borrow him once again to work in her garden. Flappy was immediately displeased. After all, she had been generous enough to offer him for a day, at her expense, it was exceedingly grasping to expect the favour to be extended to three. However, if Flappy was one thing it was astute, and she wondered, as she looked at Andy Pritchett through Molly Price's eyes, whether there was more to this than the climbing Himalayan rose. Andy was undeniably handsome. Ruggedly handsome. It might not be beyond the realm of possibility, Flappy thought as she began to appreciate just how handsome Andy Pritchett was, for Molly to have developed a crush. A Lady Chatterley-type crush. Flappy didn't blame her; after all, Jim was not the gift of laughter, was he? So, instead of saying no, she was terribly sorry but Andy was required in *her* gardens, because she had *so many* gardens and they all needed to be put to bed for the winter, she said yes.

Flappy, as previously stated, was not one to poke her nose into other people's business. It was something she would never *ever* do. But this was Andy Pritchett, *married* Andy Pritchett, Andy Pritchett who had been her gardener for over ten years, in grave danger of being lured into something illicit and dangerous by sweet (an adjective now in question) Molly Price. Therefore, it was up to Flappy, older and wiser Flappy, to investigate.

Once again, Flappy parked her car at the Bell and Dragon pub and walked up the lane until she reached the old wall that bordered Hollyberry House. Continuing on a few hundred yards she came to the place where the wall ended and iron fencing and trees took over the job of separating the property from the lane. This was her entrance. She glanced about to make sure that she wasn't going to be seen and then climbed over the fence. This was no effort for Flappy whose morning yoga sessions had given her the supple body of a much younger woman. She sprang over like a doe and made her way through the bushes until she had a clear view of the house and garden.

Flappy had dressed for the occasion just in case she was caught. She wasn't going to take any chances. She had chosen one of the many glamorous yet understated ensembles she'd bought for a trip into the South African bush some years before (only ignorant tourists used the word 'safari'. Flappy adopted the local vernacular and called it, correctly, 'bush'). She wore khaki trousers, a crisp shirt to match and a sleeveless jacket with pockets in all the right places for things like binoculars, lip salve, sun lotion and mosquito repellent. It really was a very useful jacket and now it came into use all over again as Flappy pulled out the mosquito repellent and gave her neck a good squirt. It was damp there in the bushes and full of midges.

It wasn't long before she spotted Andy. He came round the corner pushing a wheelbarrow. In the wheelbarrow, Flappy saw through her binoculars, was the climbing Himalayan rose and a spade. Andy set about digging the hole at the foot of the apple tree. Flappy didn't doubt that Molly would soon emerge and, sure enough, after a few minutes she appeared, in another floral dress and scarf, her dark hair tied up in a high ponytail. Flappy focused the binoculars and saw, as the details of Molly's face sharpened, her shining eyes and rosy cheeks and the smile that played flirtatiously about her lips. Flappy's suspicions were piqued.

Andy straightened and leaned on his spade. They began to talk. Flappy wished she could lip read. What she would have given to be able to decipher what they were saying. She didn't imagine they were talking about the climbing Himalayan rose. Their conversation was punctuated every now and then by a laugh. In fact, there was a lot of laughter. Flappy didn't imagine Molly laughed like that with Jim. She had seen Jim smile, but she wasn't sure he was even capable of laughing. Flappy knew that laughter was the way to a woman's heart. There were, to be sure, a few other ways – Flappy could vouch for those – but laughter was certainly very powerful in the winning of a woman's affection. Molly and Andy were laughing a lot.

Flappy was about to back out of the bushes when she heard the call of a familiar voice. She pressed the binoculars to her eyes and searched the garden for the person who possessed it. To her surprise, Jasper was striding across the grass. Molly waved and, when Jasper reached her, stepped onto her tiptoes to plant a kiss on his cheek. Flappy was confused. What was Jasper doing there and where was Jim? Andy and Jasper needed no introduction and the three of them chatted happily for a while.

Suddenly, Buster came trotting around the corner of the house, cocked his leg on some hellebores and then set off across the lawn in the direction of the shrubbery in which

Flappy was hiding. Jasper ignored him and continued talking to Molly and Andy. To Flappy's horror, Buster was heading straight for her. She froze. Perhaps, if she remained very still, he wouldn't notice her. However, Buster had a highly sensitive nose and, following this nose, meandered over the grass, tail wagging, getting closer and closer. He then stopped and started to bark at the bush behind which Flappy stood as still as a statue. Jasper, Molly and Andy paused their conversation and turned to look at Buster. Molly said something and laughed. Andy, Flappy imagined, was suggesting that there might be a rabbit in the bushes, and that if Buster was clever he'd catch it. Jasper called the dog back. Buster was having none of it. He saw Flappy, with his sharp canine vision (and he very likely smelled her too) and was probably wondering what she was doing there, hiding among the hazel and laurel like a thief. 'Go away!' Flappy hissed, but that only made him bark all the more excitedly.

Jasper marched towards him. 'Come on, Buster, out of there. Leave that poor rabbit alone.' Then, as he came closer, he craned his neck and narrowed his eyes. 'What have you seen in there?'

Flappy held her breath. She did not want to get caught by Jasper. She knew that, although the long-tailed skua had succeeded beautifully in fooling Mabel, it would *not* fool Jasper. He was much too clever for that.

'Come on, Buster, we've got work to do.'

At the mention of the word 'work', Flappy perked up. Jasper headed back to Molly and Andy, and the dog followed obediently after him. Flappy crept out of the bushes and retreated over the fence as quickly as she could. Her heart was beating so fast she thought it might make a break for it and burst out of her chest. She hurried down the lane, a little shaky on her legs, until she reached the safety of her car. She climbed in, closed her eyes and took a long, deep breath.

A few minutes later, just when Flappy was beginning to find a sense of calm after the storm, there came a loud tapping on the window. Flappy opened her eyes to see Mabel, Esther, Sally and Madge smiling at her through the glass. Flappy lowered the window. 'What are you doing here?' she asked, looking from one to the other in bewilderment.

'Birdwatching,' said Mabel proudly.

'At the pub?' said Flappy.

Esther gave a throaty laugh. 'No, we met here. We're on our way to the old lighthouse. Apparently, that's the place to spot the rarest birds,' she said.

Mabel took in Flappy's binoculars and was a little put out that she'd gone birdwatching without her. 'Do you want to come with us?' she asked.

Flappy could not very well say that she was busy. She thought about it a moment, trying hard to think of a reason why she couldn't join them. When nothing popped into her mind, she was left with no alternative but to go with the flow. Resisting the flow would only create friction – Murli her guru had taught her that. 'I'd love to,' she said. 'Why don't you all get in and I'll drive there.'

'Oh no,' said Mabel. 'We were hoping to spot a long-tailed skua on the way. It was just up this lane that you first spotted it, wasn't it, Flappy?'

'Indeed, it was,' said Flappy, wishing she'd never mentioned the damn bird. Reluctantly, she climbed out. Well, if she was going to spend the morning birdwatching, she might as well put as much enthusiasm into it as she put into everything else. 'Well, come on then, ladies. Let's see if we can spot the long-tailed skua.' And as she led the way back up the lane, she thought how very little she liked birdwatching.

Chapter 7

Flappy returned home at lunchtime having spotted nothing more interesting than a load of common seagulls around the old lighthouse. However, had she focused her binoculars on anything *less* common, she would not have known; Flappy was good at most things, but she was not good at recognizing the rarer types of bird. Perhaps, if Mabel had given her some notice, she might have flicked through a bird book to bone up on a few of the more exotic varieties found on the Devon coast. But she had not, so Flappy was unable to feign expertise in the field, which rendered the whole expedition pointless. She left at the earliest opportunity. As she parked her car in front of Darnley Manor, her busy mind had moved on from birds and was now returning to the place of most interest: Molly Price's garden.

Flappy was confused. Molly had certainly appeared to enjoy Andy Pritchett's company and, as far as Flappy could tell, Andy Pritchett was more intent on talking to her than planting the climbing Himalayan rose. However, Jasper's appearance had thrown her. What was *he* doing there and what was the work that he had mentioned to Buster? It was all rather baffling, but Flappy was determined to get to the bottom of it. When it came to investigating, Flappy was a dab hand. And there was nothing she enjoyed more than a good mystery.

She decided she would subtly find out what was going on from Briony.

The following morning when Briony came to swim and work out, Flappy invited her for coffee in the kitchen afterwards. 'Great,' said Briony enthusiastically. 'You can show me your sanctuary. I'm dying to do a little meditation.'

Flappy had not expected this, but what could she do? She who always had a plan, had none. 'Of course,' she replied. 'I'd love to.'

And so it was that after Briony had swum her lengths and worked out in Flappy's gym, Flappy led her down the path to the cottage, a sinking feeling in her chest because she knew that once Briony saw her shrine she would immediately want to take up the Lotus position and chant in front of it. Then it would no longer be her private place, but Briony's too and, because she was her daughter-in-law and it was imperative to maintain good relations, Flappy wouldn't be able to stop her.

Briony was, indeed, impressed with Flappy's sanctuary just as Flappy knew she would be. 'It's a slice of heaven,' she gushed, taking off her shoes at the door and padding across the carpet to admire the Buddha statue. 'This is awesome. It's jade, right?'

'Yes, it is,' said Flappy, hoping she wouldn't touch it.

Briony ran her fingers over the soft undulations of the

91

Buddha's curves. 'He's got an amazing energy. You can really feel it.' Flappy wished she wouldn't. 'So, what do you do? You light the incense, fill the room with smoke and chant?'

'Everyone meditates in their own particular way,' said Flappy. 'I like to chant. I find it takes me to a very deep place. But most people spend years trying to navigate their way to that deep place and get lost in all the mundane thoughts the mind can't let go of. It's very frustrating. But once you master it, as I have done, it's very peaceful and restorative.'

'Oh, I can meditate, no problem. My mind is only too happy to let go of all the mundane things that clutter it.' Briony put her hands on her hips and swept her eyes around the room. 'This is a gorgeous cottage. It's like a secret love nest. The sort of place where you meet your lover and no one ever finds out.'

Flappy laughed dismissively. 'You do have a rich imagination, Briony,' she said.

'I know. I should write a book.'

'That's a good idea. What's stopping you?'

'I have no staying power. I'd write the first chapter and then lose interest.'

'I have a dear friend who's a very successful novelist. I can introduce you if you like. I'm sure she can give you some helpful tips.'

'What's her name?'

'Charity Chance is her pseudonym.'

'Oh yes, she writes those sexy romcoms, doesn't she? I read one on a beach once. Brilliant.'

Flappy gave a little sniff. 'I wouldn't know.'

Briony looked surprised. 'She's your friend and you've never read one of her books?'

'They're just not my thing.'

'How would you know if you've never tried one?'

Flappy did not like to be challenged. 'I've dipped in,' she replied tightly.

Briony grinned. 'I bet you secretly enjoyed it.'

'If I had, I wouldn't keep it a secret. I'd be the first to say how much I enjoyed it.'

'I think you should give her another go. Firstly, because she's your friend and secondly, because I think you would really enjoy them. You can't read Dostoevsky all the time, you know.'

Flappy had never read Dostoevsky, but she wasn't going to admit that. She rather loved having the image of someone who read the Russian Greats.

Flappy decided that now was as good a moment as any to mention Molly Price. 'I see you've met the Prices,' she said breezily, sweeping her fingers over the windowsill in search of non-existent dust to give the impression that she was only mildly interested in the subject.

'Yes, we did,' Briony replied. '*She's* sweet. *He's* kind of mysterious.'

'How so?' Flappy asked. She saw no mystery there, only lack of humour and vim.

Briony grinned. 'He's secretive.'

'I thought him a little cold when I met him. But I'm sure Jasper will warm him up. Jasper's humour is so infectious, isn't it?'

Briony laughed. 'Yes, everyone loves Jasper.'

'Still, it's nice to have found some young people in town. They have children of the same age as yours, don't they?'

'Yeah, Molly's a sweetheart. I might ask her if she wants to work out with me.'

Flappy's breath caught in her chest. An image of Molly and Briony in Lycra, working out in her gym, crashed across her mind like a herd of elephants. 'Oh, I think she looks more like a yoga girl, don't you?'

'Sure, I can do yoga. It would be nice to do it with a friend.'

Flappy swallowed. This was not going the way she had intended. 'There must be a yoga class in town you can join. Such fun to do it with lots of other young people. I'll ask Persephone. She'll know. Persephone knows everything.'

'She's nice too. She and George,' said Briony. Flappy thought the danger might have passed and took a breath. 'Maybe she can join our yoga class. The three of us. You wouldn't mind us using your gym, would you? I mean, Kenneth told me you only use it at five in the morning. Five in the morning, Flappy? You're crazy! I couldn't drag myself up at five. Even when the children were tiny I couldn't get out of bed. Jasper did all the morning wake-ups for me.'

'Jasper's a saint,' said Flappy. The more she knew of Briony, the more she realized just how much of a saint Jasper was.

'We'll come in via the side door so we don't disturb you.'

Flappy was now feeling giddy with the slipperiness of the slope down which she felt she was swiftly falling. There was no stopping Briony, who, to Flappy's dismay, had no sense of Flappy's position in this town, no sense of deference, no trepidation. With one look, Flappy could slice through every heart in Badley Compton if she so wanted, which she most often didn't because Flappy was a woman who knew very well that a light touch was more effective than a heavy hammer. But Briony was unafraid, as if she thought Flappy was something of a joke. In the space of only a week she had inveigled her way into Flappy's swimming pool, her gym, her gardens and her sanctuary, and was now wangling Molly's way in there as well.

The two women wandered slowly back up the garden path. Briony admired the muted colours of autumn, while Flappy was eager to reassert her position on top. 'I've lent Molly one of my gardeners, Andy Pritchett, who's such a pro,' she said. 'Their garden needs an awful lot of work, I believe.'

'That's good of you. Molly told me that one of the reasons they've moved down here is that life is less expensive in the country.'

'Is that so,' said Flappy. 'Hollyberry House is hardly modest, though, is it.'

'It's a proper home. One day we'll have a proper home like that,' said Briony with confidence and Flappy pursed her lips and did not agree, for that is what Briony wanted: her agreement, and Kenneth's money to buy it.

'Has Jasper seen it?' Flappy asked, then aware that her question was a little odd, she added, 'He's always loved gardens.' Which was true; Jasper loved everything.

'We had a drink with them the other night,' said Briony.

'How lovely,' Flappy replied, wondering with even more curiosity whether Briony knew that Jasper had been in Molly's garden and what he was doing there.

'I'm sure they're grateful that you've lent them Andy. Your gardens are legendary.'

At that compliment, so genuinely given, Flappy felt a little better. 'Thank you, Briony, that's kind of you.'

'No, really. The gardens at Darnley are really wonderful. I'm not a gardener. I'd hate to get my hands dirty and I know nothing about plants. But I know what's beautiful and what isn't, and the gardens here are awesome. But you have beautiful taste, Flappy. Everything you do, you do with style.'

Flappy inhaled through her nostrils and smelled the sweet putrefaction of summer's bounty with pleasure. 'I would be delighted if you and your girlfriends use my gym for yoga,' she said, suddenly feeling warm towards her daughter-in-law. 'Perhaps you can find someone to take the lesson. Ask Persephone. She'll know.'

'She's great,' Briony agreed.

'I know, I'm so *so* lucky to have a PA.' And, as Flappy focused on her good fortune, her spirits lifted and the two women settled happily in the kitchen for a cosy cup of coffee.

Flappy did not expect Briony to bring Molly to Darnley so soon, but arrive they did, at nine the following morning, armed with yoga mats and water bottles and dressed in Lycra leggings and loose tops, their hair tied up in high ponytails. Flappy watched them get out of Molly's blue BMW four by four from her bedroom window, which had the advantage of two views, one of the front, the other of the croquet lawn. The two women were chatting excitedly, as if they had known each other all their lives. Flappy didn't think they were going to get much yoga done. But she wasn't about to go down and spy on them. Flappy abhorred spying.

However, after about half an hour Flappy went out into the garden to take a break from her exceedingly busy morning. Persephone was occupied with all the arrangements for the jumble sale and the Harvest Festival tea. The Harvest Festival tea was really for the children and Flappy had invited Hedda to judge the pumpkin competition, which she had accepted without hesitation. Before Hedda had come to live in Badley Compton, Lady Micklethwaite had been the guest of honour at Flappy's events, cutting ribbons and saying a few well-chosen words of welcome which, coming from a Lady, were gratefully received. Now she had left Compton Court and gone to live in Spain, Hedda, the niece of a marquess, had taken her place as the town aristocrat – Flappy could claim many titles, but not that one. She was mightily relieved. After all, had Hedda not moved into Compton Court, who would Flappy have roped in to do the honours? Of course, *she* could have bowed to public pressure and taken up the mantle herself, but she was, deep down, a humble and unassuming woman who knew very well that she was better backstage, not front of house. However, had they insisted . . .

There she was in the garden, the pool garden to be precise, wandering about busily clipping a dead rose here and pulling out a weed there, when she saw, through the glass, Briony and Molly sitting on the edge of the pool, chatting. She wondered whether they had actually done any yoga at all. She paused her labours – even though she had a wonderful team of professionals to maintain her garden she was a perfectionist and therefore couldn't resist pruning the odd shrub – and thought how happy the two of them looked, laughing like old friends. Flappy's mind turned to Persephone then and she wondered whether *she* might like to join them. After all, they were of a similar age and Briony had agreed that Persephone was 'great'. Persephone might also be a handy spy. With that in mind she went back to the house to graciously allow her PA some time off.

Persephone was on the telephone to Big Mary when Flappy walked into the library, arranging cakes for the Harvest Festival tea. Flappy waited until she had hung up and then perched on the edge of the sofa and crossed her legs. 'You know my daughter-in-law Briony and Molly Price who's just moved into Hollyberry House are using the pool and gym this morning.'

Persephone looked surprised. 'No, I wasn't aware of that. Are you happy that they're using your facilities?'

'Delighted. After all, I use the gym at five in the morning, the rest of the day the place is empty. I'm so *so* lucky to have such a lovely spa, it's the least I can do to share it.'

Persephone was relieved. 'Oh, good. I just know that sometimes you're too generous to say no and then regret it.'

Flappy smiled. 'You're absolutely right. However, I do hate to disappoint people. So, when Briony asked to bring Molly

I couldn't very well say no. Neither has a pool or a gym, so what could I do but say yes?'

'I'm sure they're very grateful.'

'I'm sure they are.' Flappy didn't think Briony was at all grateful. She couldn't guess at Molly. 'Briony mentioned *you* and asked whether you'd like to join them. I just wanted to tell you that I'd be delighted if you did. They arrived at nine for yoga and then had a swim. It'll be fun and it would be nice for them to get to know someone from Badley Compton who's their own age.'

'I could take it as my lunch hour, or stay an extra hour at the end of the day,' Persephone suggested.

'You really don't need to. I'm very happy for you to take some time off. You do work very hard.'

'There you go again, Flappy, allowing your good nature to be abused. I would love to join them for yoga but I won't swim and I'll make up the time at the end of the day.'

'You're a good girl,' said Flappy, feeling strangely moved. There was something so wonderfully wholesome about Persephone. 'Why don't you go down now. See if they want a cup of coffee or something, and find out whether they're coming tomorrow. It's Saturday, after all, so you could take as long as you like.'

Persephone got up. 'I'll be quick. I've got loads to do.' And she hastily left the room.

Oh, thought Flappy with a sigh. *If only my daughters Charlotte and Mathilda were as sweet and good-natured as Persephone.*

Over the following week Persephone joined Briony and Molly every morning for yoga in the gym at nine. Flappy found that, far from resenting her daughter-in-law for stridently taking possession of her spa, she rather relished having them there. The house was, if she was honest, rather quiet. So quiet, in fact, that she could hear the tick-tock of the grandfather clock in the hall, even when she was in her study, which was quite a distance, the house being so very big. It pleased her to think of the spa being used and enjoyed, rather than remaining for the greater part of the day like a museum, beautiful but empty. She wasn't at all surprised to find that after they'd left, the place was clean and tidy. She imagined Persephone had seen to that. Wonderful Persephone.

Flappy was grateful for the sunshine when the day of the jumble sale arrived. A tent had been erected on the flat surface of the croquet lawn where, in the days when Flappy and Kenneth's children had been young, endless games had been played with their friends. But those days were long gone now and the lawn hadn't seen a hoop or a mallet in at least ten years. It was the perfect location for a tent and Flappy made good use of it. Barely a month went by when there wasn't some sort of festivity. Today, being a Saturday, the entire town had turned up, as it always did. As Flappy knew it would. Her events had a sparkle, an allure, and a frisson of excitement always rippled through the community when the great day arrived. Today was no exception. Even though it was a jumble sale there was champagne, smoked salmon on brown bread crowned with a small but satisfying garnish of caviar, and macaroons, as if it were a glamorous party, and moving among the women, like a fox in a hen house, was Charles. Flappy knew it would be wise to avoid him, especially as Hedda was present, so she turned her attention to the stalls.

Flappy was careful these days to mix her own second-hand things with everyone else's. For many years she had had a whole table to herself with a couple of rails for her clothes, but the excitement had been such that a terrible stampede had ensued as the women of Badley Compton squabbled like gannets around a shoal of shimmering fish in their desperation to get to her table. Meanwhile, the other tables, laden with less dazzling items, languished like soggy pieces of bread in which the gannets had little interest. Flappy had found the whole experience mortifying and decided, after a few disastrous years, to mix it all up. Now the gannets picked at everything, seeking to distinguish Flappy's things from everyone else's. It wasn't difficult. After all, Flappy's cast-offs were of a far superior quality and easily identifiable.

As Flappy glided around the tables, she was aware of Charles's gaze upon her. It gave her a frisson of pleasure to feel the heat of his desire and she suddenly grew more animated and infinitely more charming, finding the right thing to say to everyone. Once or twice their eyes met across the crowded marquee and Flappy noticed the curl on his lips — those soft, sensual lips that had gently parted to kiss her. She took a breath, averted her gaze and tried to concentrate on Mabel, who was now talking to her.

'It's going terribly well, isn't it?' said Mabel breathlessly, happy to find Flappy on her own. 'I think we're going to raise more money than last year.'

'I think you're probably right,' said Flappy, spotting her grandson Tom pulling a toy train off the children's table and then diving beneath the cloth to play with it. 'People really are so generous, aren't they?'

'It gets bigger every year.'

'What started as a small event selling people's rejects has now become more of a Christmas fair, don't you think?'

'As long as it raises money for a good cause, I don't think it matters. Tell me, how's your New Year ball going?'

Flappy was pleased to be asked. She was immensely excited about her *ballo in maschera*. 'Badley Compton won't have seen anything like it, Mabel.'

'Is it wildly extravagant?'

Flappy gave a sniff to show her displeasure and lowered her voice. 'You know I never *ever* talk about money, it's frightfully common, but between you and me, Mabel, it's costing a fortune.'

Mabel was suitably impressed. 'And Kenneth?'

'Is only too happy to dig deep into his pockets.' Flappy smiled, trying not to look smug. Smugness, she believed, was just as common as talking about money. 'I'm so *so* lucky to have Kenneth.' Saying Kenneth's name out loud focused her mind on her marriage and she felt a pang of guilt for having imagined Charles kissing her. But the focus didn't last for long, nor did her guilt, for her eyes strayed once again across the room in search of him. However, it wasn't Charles she spotted through the small gaps between people and their wares, but Jasper and Molly, who were deep in conversation. Indeed, their heads were close together and they were whispering, as if sharing a secret. Flappy was struck by the intimacy of their body language. What on earth were they whispering about?

Then Molly did something that turned Flappy's heart to ice. She held Jasper's face in her hands and looked up at him lovingly. Jasper laughed. Flappy was appalled. It reminded her of the many times Charles had held *her* face like that and looked into *her* eyes with equal affection, and lust – yes, lust, certainly at the beginning, had outweighed affection. Flappy also recalled how very quickly they had fallen onto each other like wild animals and made love in the changing room of the pool house. Flappy knew more than anyone how swiftly an affair can start. Were Jasper and Molly having an affair?

'Are you all right, Flappy?' asked Mabel, noticing her features suddenly darken.

'That devil of a grandson of mine has helped himself to a toy train and is now playing with it beneath the table,' Flappy replied in a smooth deflection.

'Where's his mother?'

'That's a very good question, Mabel,' said Flappy, and, as she glanced through the crowd at her son and Molly, a steely determination glinted in her eyes. 'That's a very good question, indeed.'

'Flappy.' It was Charles.

Flappy was startled. She had not expected him to pounce from behind. She swung round. 'Charles.'

'Flappy,' he said again. Flappy glanced at the spot where Mabel had been standing to find it empty. Mabel was now eagerly pursuing a tray of smoked salmon sandwiches. Charles looked into her eyes. 'You never stop,' he said in a soft voice, brimming with admiration. 'You're always busy doing things for other people. It's time you did something for yourself. You deserve to be spoiled.' He grinned wickedly and Flappy's heart melted like an ice cream in sunshine. 'And I know exactly how to spoil you.'

'Charles, you have to be careful. Hedda—'

'Is at the other end of the marquee, buying Christmas presents for her godchildren. She has eleven, so she'll be some time.' His gaze caressed the contours of her face, then lingered on her lips.

Flappy parted them with a gasp. 'Oh, Charles.'

'You cannot turn off our chemistry with a switch. It is always there, vibrating in the air between us, like heat off a hot tin roof. Every time I look at you, Beauty, I feel it.'

'Oh, Charles,' said Flappy again, because she didn't know what else to say. She felt her grip on control loosen. Seeing Jasper and Molly sharing a secret moment had set her off balance.

'My body aches for you, my darling. I think I'll go mad.'

Flappy was grateful that she wasn't alone with him. Had it not been for the two hundred people gathered in the marquee and Hedda, lingering over Christmas presents, she might have given in and allowed him to do all the delicious things he'd listed in that note. *Oh, for one more afternoon of pleasure . . .*

'Flappy!' It was Joan. Flappy blushed. She knew without a doubt that the sudden appearance of the vicar's wife was God's intervention, saving her from herself.

'Joan, how lovely you could make it,' she said, gathering herself. When she turned back to Charles, she found that he had gone.

Chapter 8

That night Flappy was unable to sleep. Kenneth lay beside her, grunting and twitching beneath the covers, dreaming no doubt of the ever elusive 'hole in one'. Flappy wished that she had as little to worry about as her husband. But her busy mind was plagued with conundrums. Really, she didn't think there was a busier person in the whole of Badley Compton. The thing that worried her the most was not Charles – Charles was not a worry, he was a forbidden pleasure she had so far managed to resist. No, what worried her the most was Jasper and Molly's secret friendship – and secret it surely was for Briony seemed to have no idea he'd been to Hollyberry House on his own, without her. Flappy could hardly mention it to her son, for then she'd have to admit that she'd been hiding in the bushes with her binoculars, spying – something she would never *ever* do, unless ... No, she could not talk directly to Jasper until she had concrete proof of something underhand. And Flappy knew all about underhand, having been underhand herself.

Flappy was a woman with a sharp and steady moral compass. A woman who could be counted upon to be honest and true. In fact, she prided herself (if she could allow herself a moment's self-indulgence) on being the moral paragon of Badley Compton. Someone everyone looked up to to set an example, to lead, to show them how things must be done. Flappy, although almost too good to be true, was, nevertheless, a woman of flesh and blood like any other and she too had her faults. Few, to be sure, but faults nonetheless. Her affair with Charles had been a mistake, a very pleasant mistake, but a mistake all the same and one she was not going to repeat. Nevertheless, her experience had opened her eyes to the less savoury pursuits of the wider population and made her more adept at recognizing them. After all, it takes one to know one. With this in mind, she asked herself again, could Jasper be having an affair with Molly? Was it possible to embark on such a thing so soon after having met? Well, Flappy knew the answer to that. When desire is hot, it's hot.

What was she going to do about it? This question kept her heart rate pounding more than any other because Flappy was a woman who liked to get things done. When there was a problem, she sorted it. At once. Straight away. She didn't like things to linger unresolved. But this was not something she could sort, at any rate, not immediately. Firstly, she wasn't sure they really were having an affair. Secondly, if she *was* sure and confronted Jasper about it, she knew her son well enough to know that he would simply smile and deny it, as would Molly. No, they had to be caught in the act. But how?

Kenneth snorted loudly and turned over, taking most

of the sheet and eiderdown with him – Flappy did not like duvets, they were common, like electric blankets and Teasmades. A proper bed should be made with linen, blankets and eiderdowns, hot water bottles and cups of tea brought up from the kitchen on trays, the old-fashioned way. As Kenneth settled like a pig in hay, she considered telling him about her conundrum. Kenneth, in spite of her comparing him (affectionately) to a pig or a toad, was surprisingly sensitive in delicate matters such as this. She recalled the times they'd discussed their children's love affairs and broken hearts as they'd navigated their way through the thorny thicket of adolescence. Kenneth had always been sensible, understanding and wise. However, he was innocent when it came to extramarital affairs. For a start, as far as she knew, and she really *did* think she knew very well, Kenneth had never had one. He was much too obsessed with his golf to have either the time or the inclination to stray from the marital bed, or the golf club for that matter. He would be appalled to hear that his golden son, for he really *did* consider Jasper to be golden, was behaving badly and most likely would disbelieve it. Flappy watched his breath rising and falling peacefully from beneath the White Company linen, and her heart went out to him. What sort of woman would she be if she burdened *him* with this worry that was burdening *her*? Surely, if she had any compassion at all, she would shield him from it. Protect him from the ugliness of what lay beyond his perception and allow him to enjoy his golf without undue stress.

What's more, the fewer people who knew about it, the

better. Flappy did not want to be dragged into Jasper's reflected shame!

No, she would not discuss it with Kenneth. She would not discuss it with Mabel or Hedda. She would keep it to herself. Nevertheless, there was one person who deserved her sympathy and tacit support. Briony. However annoying she was, and she was, really, very annoying, Flappy would make a greater effort to be nice.

Late October brought cold winds and damp weather. The sunshine that had blazed through the early part of the month lost its vigour, distracted no doubt by the lure of spring on the other side of the world. Its head was well and truly turned and would not be tempted back for another six months, at least. Wet clouds advanced over the sea and settled over the land, releasing rain in deluges onto the sodden fields below. Flappy's gardens grew soggy and yet the gardeners toiled on, undeterred by the inclement weather for, as Flappy so rightly said, a gardener's life is in the elements, whatever they may be. There was no reprieve for them, but Flappy abandoned her secateurs and only ventured outside to walk to her car.

Always one to look on the bright side, Flappy enjoyed the change of season because it meant a whole new wardrobe of clothes to choose from. Out came the three-ply cashmere, the flannel trousers, the tweed. She was able to wear her tailored jackets once again and embellish them with Hermès scarves. Tired now of white linen and pearl grey, she reverted to gentle beiges and charcoal grey, black lace and fur (expensive faux fur, for it was a definite no-no to wear real fur). Flappy was delighted that the temperature had dropped for she could light the fires in the drawing room and hall, bring out the cinnamon-scented candles, wrap herself in soft fabrics, and embrace winter in all its cosy luxury. Darnley did cosy exceedingly well; in fact, Flappy didn't think there was a house in Badley Compton that did cosy as well as Darnley, not even Compton Court with all Hedda's inherited Persian rugs and soft furnishings.

It was in this cocoon of cashmere and open fires that Flappy hosted her dinner parties, her lunches, her book club meetings and her coffee mornings for the various committees she chaired. Persephone was always on hand to take notes, make tea, pour the wine and generally support Flappy who considered it very chic to have a PA and showed her off at every opportunity.

Flappy had permitted Andy to help Molly with her garden on seven occasions now. Seven. For nothing. Not a penny. Flappy might have been a bit peeved had it not been for the fact that Andy had revealed, in the car en route to the garden centre, that Jasper had turned up *again* and suggested Molly plant an orchard of apple trees where in the old days there had apparently been a large vegetable garden. 'Since when is Jasper such an expert on gardening?' Flappy asked, knowing that if she was going to get information out of Andy without looking like she was prying, she was going to have to be subtle about it.

'It was a good suggestion,' Andy replied. 'It's land that's lying idle.'

Flappy slowed the Range Rover as she neared a bend in the road. 'I see Jasper and Briony are becoming good friends of the Prices.'

'That's nice, both families being new in town,' he said.

'It is, very nice,' Flappy agreed, hoping Andy would give her a little more information on Jasper. He did not. 'Did Jasper turn up simply to help Molly with her garden?' she asked smoothly. 'Careful, or he'll be doing you out of a job soon,' she joked.

Andy chuckled. He knew Jasper was no threat to him. 'I don't think so. He just arrived when we were discussing what to do with it and decided to add his two and six.'

'Typical Jasper,' Flappy said with a smile. 'Full of suggestions about everything.' *But never actually doing anything himself,* she thought bitterly. 'Where's Jim in all of this? Is *he* interested in the garden?'

'He's a bit like Mr Scott-Booth,' Andy replied. 'He probably likes it to look nice, but doesn't want to have to bother himself with the details.'

Jim is nothing like Kenneth, Flappy thought, *because Kenneth pays — and Kenneth has a sense of humour.*

'Is he busy working?' Flappy asked, trying to ascertain whether Molly and Jasper were alone in the house.

'Very busy, apparently. He's rarely at home these days. Molly says he's found an office in town and is in it for most of the day.'

Ah, and there it is, thought Flappy. *Jim and the children out of the house while Molly and Jasper get up to goodness knows what.* And because of that important piece of information,

111

Flappy had allowed Andy to work in Molly's garden for the eighth time.

Flappy was busy at the island in the kitchen, finalizing the guest list for her *ballo in maschera,* when the doorbell went. She didn't so much as raise an eyebrow because Persephone was there to answer it. Flappy's pen hovered over the names as she contemplated including people she didn't really want to include – whether the offence caused by her not inviting them would outweigh her annoyance at having them there. She was just about to draw a line through one of these annoying couples when Persephone appeared in the doorway. 'Molly's here to see you, Flappy.'

Flappy raised her eyes over her reading glasses. 'Molly?' She didn't recall having booked Molly into her diary.

Persephone lowered her voice. 'She's got a gift for you.'

Flappy put down her pen and took off her glasses. 'Really? Well, you'd better show her in then.' She closed her Smythson leather writing folder and waited. A moment later Molly entered with a stunning glass bowl of six white orchids. 'What is this?' Flappy exclaimed in delight, moving *The Times* that Kenneth had left on the island to make room for it. 'What beautiful orchids! My favourite.'

Molly was pleased. 'The lady in the flower shop suggested them. She obviously knows what you like.'

Flappy made a mental note to include Cynthia on the party list. 'She certainly does. How lovely. But what's the occasion?'

'I wanted to thank you for letting us borrow Andy.'

'It's a pleasure,' said Flappy, waving her manicured fingers in the air to show that it was really nothing for a woman who had a whole team of gardeners at her disposal.

'He's wonderful. So efficient. In half a day he does what a normal gardener would do in a week.'

'Yes, I am so *so* lucky to have such a competent gardener to lead my team.' Flappy slipped off her stool. 'Would you like a cup of coffee? I'm going to have another. You can keep me company.'

'Oh, thank you. I'd love one,' said Molly.

'Do sit down. Milk? Sugar?'

'Black, please. I like my coffee strong.' Molly settled herself on one of the stools.

'Me too,' said Flappy, putting the espresso cup in the machine and pressing a button. 'Andy tells me you're going to plant an orchard.'

'Yes, it's a lovely idea. I'll be able to make apple pie out of my own apples. The kids will love that.' Flappy flinched at the word 'kids', but didn't correct her. She did lament the fact that the younger generation didn't know how to speak properly.

'Was that Andy's idea or yours?' Flappy asked, bringing her cup of coffee to the island.

'It was Jasper's idea, actually,' said Molly.

'Really?' 'Hiding in plain sight' popped into Flappy's busy mind.

'Yes, we've been seeing a lot of Jasper and Briony. Our kids are at the same school, even in the same classes, so

113

we alternate pick-ups and drop-offs and arrange playdates together. It works really well. I'm lucky they chose to move here at the same time we did.'

'I'm so pleased,' said Flappy, wondering if Molly was going to mention Jasper's solo visits to her house.

'We've also been seeing George and Persephone, when George comes down on weekends.'

'Is that right? How lovely that George is spending more time in Badley Compton.'

'He wants to find a job here.'

'Does he, indeed. Well, I hope he finds one. He'd make his mother very happy, and Persephone, of course. Long-distance relationships are hard to maintain.' Flappy sat down with her espresso adjacent to Molly. 'Tell me, how's Jim's work going?'

'Well. He's busy. He's rented an office at last because he says there are too many distractions at home.'

Flappy laughed. 'How lovely to have the whole house to yourself.'

'It's certainly better for the marriage.'

'Is it?'

'Yes. Things were getting tense in London, the house not being very big and us getting on top of each other.' Molly lowered her eyes and Flappy sensed that things were not well in their marriage. Not well at all.

'Oh dear,' she said, giving Molly a sympathetic smile. The kind of smile that inspires trust.

'To be honest,' Molly replied in a confiding tone, 'Jim's been depressed.'

'What, properly depressed?'

'Yes, it's been hard. Have you ever had to live with someone who wanders around beneath a permanent black cloud?'

'No, I haven't,' Flappy admitted. Kenneth skipped about beneath a permanent rainbow.

'Well, it's tough.'

'I did notice he was a teeny bit quiet at Hedda's dinner.'

Molly rolled her eyes and sighed heavily. 'I was mortified,' she confessed. 'There I was talking like a madwoman to compensate for his monosyllabic responses and he wasn't even trying. It was horrendous.'

'I'm so sorry,' said Flappy, who really did feel *very* sorry. 'Is it any better now that you've settled in?'

Molly took a sip of coffee and Flappy could tell from the way she no longer hunched over her cup that confiding in a friend had made her feel better. A problem shared is a problem halved, Flappy thought with satisfaction. 'The fact that he has rented an office has made a big difference,' Molly told her. 'He's a changed person. The cloud has lifted. He's getting lots of commissions and things are really picking up. It hasn't just made a difference to him, but to me too. I feel I can breathe again. I don't have this dark presence in the house all day. I don't have to tiptoe around the place in fear of disturbing him, or saying the wrong thing. And then Jasper and Briony have been brilliant. Jasper makes him laugh. I didn't think anyone could make Jim laugh.'

'Jasper is quite a character.' Flappy noticed Molly's eyes light up.

'He really is. He's just so funny, and kind.'

115

'I'm so *so* lucky to have such a kind son. He's wonderful to me,' which wasn't entirely true, but it sounded good. 'I'm looking forward to him finding a job. He was an entrepreneur in Australia, you know. I'm sure he'll start a business over here. He's got the Midas touch.' Again, not an ounce of truth, but Flappy was on a roll now. 'He's so secretive, though. He doesn't tell me anything. He waits until it's all in the bag before he makes the grand announcement. I'm waiting, with bated breath, for that moment to come.'

'I'm sure he'll make a success of whatever he puts his hand to. He's clearly talented,' said Molly.

Flappy smiled, wondering what exactly his talent was besides charming people. Perhaps that in itself was a talent which could be put to good use. 'And you, Molly? What are *you* up to?'

'I'm painting again,' said Molly. By the bashful look on her face, Flappy didn't imagine she was very good at it.

'Painting? I thought you wrote.'

'I did, but I'm trying something new. I went to art college, but then turned to writing. It was an easier way to make money.'

'Painting is a lovely hobby. I used to paint. I turned the little cottage we have at the bottom of the garden into a studio, but in the end, after having an exhibition of my work, which was surprisingly successful considering that I was an amateur, I just didn't have the time. I gave up.'

'Oh, that's a shame.'

'Yes, it was. So many people bought my paintings and hung them on their walls and, I might add, tried to convince me to continue, but I was compelled to disappoint. One can't spread oneself so thinly or one does nothing properly.'

'I've converted one of the rooms at home into a studio.' Molly smiled and put down her empty coffee cup. 'It's making me feel good. I might not make any money, but I'm making *myself* happy.'

'That's the spirit,' said Flappy. 'Painting and gardening are wonderfully healing for the soul.'

'And yoga,' Molly added. 'Since doing yoga with Briony and Persephone every morning, I'm really feeling like a new person.'

'I'm glad,' said Flappy, who really was, *very* glad. Molly had turned out to be completely different from the pushy usurper she had taken her for, and Flappy felt bad about that. She had misjudged her, to be sure. But Flappy was nothing if not magnanimous. When it came to U-turns, she was the first to admit that she was very good at them.

And so it was, when Briony asked Flappy if she and Molly could use her cottage to meditate at her shrine, Flappy said yes. There were one or two conditions, of course, for not only did Flappy use the room herself – very occasionally, it must be acknowledged – but she and her ladies used it on Thursday evenings for yoga and meditation as a group, led by Flappy's guru Murli. This was sacred time and everyone at Darnley knew not to disturb them.

Briony agreed to use the cottage two evenings a week and to avoid Thursdays. 'You're incredibly kind to let me use your home,' she said, and Flappy felt so good about herself, because it really would be only too easy to keep the wonders of Darnley to herself, that she replied:

'You're my daughter-in-law, Briony. Darnley is your home as much as it is mine.' She hoped Briony wouldn't take that literally and extend her use of it any further. The pool, the gym, the gardens and the cottage were as much as Flappy was prepared to share. And share it she did, not only because Briony was married to Jasper and because she was particularly generous, but also because she felt sorry for Briony. If Jasper was, indeed, behaving badly with Molly, it was the least she could do, as his mother, to give her tacit support to his wife.

Chapter 9

Darnley was slowly becoming a hub of activity. The once peaceful grounds of Flappy's beautiful home rang out with the sound of children playing, Buster barking and cars arriving and leaving. Not only were Briony and Molly constant visitors, but Jasper was also making the most of the tennis court. For a man supposedly looking for a job, he seemed to spend a great deal of time having fun. During the week he played with Charles, who claimed that the court at Compton was being treated for moss and was therefore unusable. Thus the two of them played on the court at Darnley, which had no such affliction, and on the weekends Jasper played with George. When he wasn't playing tennis, he was on the golf course with his father and his father's cronies. There didn't seem to be any time left for job hunting; at least, not that Flappy could discern. Life for Jasper seemed just fine and dandy.

When it came to Charles, Flappy knew exactly why he insisted on playing tennis at Darnley. He hoped he could win her back. He had said as much and, as Flappy had discovered during those few torrid weeks of their affair, he was a man of his word. However, he had not counted on Flappy's resolve or her loyalty to his wife. He rolled up in his Bentley, in perfect white tennis shorts and shirt, a white cricket sweater draped casually over his shoulders, and either wandered into the hall and shouted for her, or went around the side of the house and rapped upon her study window. Either way, Flappy responded graciously, because she was, at heart, a gracious woman, and it went against her nature to be discourteous. However, she did not really like to be surprised. Flappy, admittedly, did not do surprises well. Nevertheless, she greeted him politely, tried to keep him at arm's length and reminded herself over and over of all the things she would lose were she to give in to even one small kiss. As tempting as it was, and it was, certainly, *very* tempting, Flappy had made up her mind.

Flappy was not alone in her struggle. Persephone, the sensitive young woman that she was, soon picked up on Flappy's awkward predicament and rose to the occasion like a guardian angel, saving Flappy from herself as well as from Charles. Rarely was there a time when Flappy had to face Charles alone. Persephone always seemed to walk in at just the moment he appeared at Flappy's study window or when he let himself into the hall. And Persephone, being his son George's girlfriend, could not be dismissed as one could dismiss ordinary staff.

However, there was, unfortunately, the odd occasion when Persephone had to go into town on an errand, leaving

Flappy dangerously exposed. It was on one such occasion that Flappy, without protection, nearly came undone.

It was a particularly splendid October afternoon and Flappy was in the pool house watering the orchids. She had managed to avoid Charles by hiding out upstairs in her bedroom. Believing herself quite safe, she was humming a tune and admiring the beautiful room, drenched as it was in golden autumnal light, when she heard the door open and softly close. She turned round to see Charles in his tennis whites. 'Flappy,' he said.

'Charles,' she replied, startled. She had not expected him to turn up here. He usually went straight home after the game.

'I've come for a swim,' he told her, smiling broadly, like a fox who has stolen into the chicken coop.

Flappy put down the watering can. She noticed he was not carrying his leather holdall and guessed that he hadn't come down here with the intention of swimming at all. 'Then I will leave you to your swim,' she said. But in order to do that she had to walk past him. She did not want to go through the garden in her light-coloured suede shoes. Charles watched her, that smile revealing in its mischievous curl all the naughty things he planned to do to her. There was a glint of intent in his eyes too. An expectant look on his face. Flappy had seen that look before. It had excited her then and it excited her now. She caught her breath. She knew she was walking into a trap but she couldn't stop herself.

When she reached him he put his hand against the wall, preventing her from accessing the door. He looked down at her. Flappy gazed into the hypnotic green and felt a sense of drowning, of helplessness, of delicious surrender. For how much longer could she contain the beast within, when that beast had tasted the forbidden pleasures of Charles's love-making and was now rattling its cage for more? She looked up at Charles and bit her lip. He held her chin between his finger and thumb and lifted her face towards him. She parted her lips. He lowered his. As his mouth hovered above hers, sending a shock of aching desire coursing through her loins, she closed her eyes and anticipated the kiss. Just as he was about to uncage the beast the door opened and a group of noisy children burst in.

Flappy was wrenched out of her trance with a jolt. Knowing that she must give some sort of explanation for their proximity, she said in a voice as serene as summer, 'Can you see what it is in my eye, Charles? Don't worry, I'll give it a good wash and whatever it is will probably come out on its own.' She laughed carelessly, as if it were the most normal thing in the world for Charles's mouth to be hovering an inch above hers. 'Hello, children.'

Charles stepped back. 'Water, yes,' he said and coughed awkwardly. 'That'll do the trick.' He looked at the children in bewilderment as they hurried into the changing rooms.

A moment later Kim appeared with a bagful of plastic toys. 'Hello, Mrs Scott-Booth,' she said in a cheerful voice.

'Hello, Kim,' Flappy replied with equal cheerfulness. If there was one thing Flappy was good at, it was smiling in the face of disappointment. And she was, to be sure, *deeply* disappointed. She turned to Charles. 'Still want to swim?' she asked.

'I think I'll go home and take a cold shower instead,' he mumbled and she watched him leave the pool house, closing the door behind him with a bang.

Darnley was thrust into the centre of things. At first, Flappy wasn't quite sure how she felt about it. Being incredibly busy, it was a distraction to have so much going on. On top of Jasper, his family and friends coming and going, Flappy hosted meetings in her drawing room – the parish meetings, book club meetings, charity meetings, church maintenance meetings among many others, so that on some days the front of the house looked like a municipal car park. Car parks were very common and Flappy wasn't happy to have her gravel churned up beneath so many wheels or, indeed, for the front of the house, which was such a showpiece, to be obscured by vehicles. However, by and by she began to rather enjoy the activity. When her children were young Darnley had teemed with people, then they had left and the place had gone quiet. Now it was noisy again and there was something rather nice about that. It made her feel wanted, in demand, popular, and if Flappy enjoyed one thing more than any other, it was being popular.

There was also another advantage to Darnley being at the centre of things. Flappy, with her eagle eye and sharp powers of observation, could watch from the sidelines as the various relationships developed. Persephone and George's was blossoming like a cherry tree in spring. On weekends, Persephone sat on the bench beside the tennis court and watched George play Jasper, then, when the game was over and they came in for a drink, Flappy would observe the tender looks the two of them gave one another and the affectionate hand-holding and subtle caresses that went on when they thought no one was looking. And the more she looked, the more she wanted very badly for George to move to Badley Compton. She did not want to lose Persephone. However, of one thing she was certain, those two lovebirds were *not* going to lose each other.

Flappy also had the opportunity to watch Jasper and Molly interact with each other because Jasper invited the Prices to come to Darnley for games of croquet. It had been years since anyone had touched a mallet, but out came the green box, all dusty and weathered from the mower shed where it was kept with the tennis ball machine and barrels of balls, and set out on the lawn. Flappy was, indeed, rather moved when she saw it. She recalled those balmy summer evenings when the light was golden and the midges lit up like fireflies, as the children and their friends played croquet and tennis, lay chatting on the lawn, while Kenneth handed around glass tumblers of Pimm's, garnished with strawberries and mint leaves, and everything was as perfect as a Ralph Lauren advert.

Flappy watched from her bedroom window, unseen, and was filled with a bittersweet nostalgia. How fast the years went by, she thought. How quickly one's present became one's past, never to be recaptured, lost but to memory, to bask in with fond regret. She swept her eyes over the garden below, distracted suddenly by the gilded leaves and retreating plants, and felt all too keenly the draining away of autumn and the approaching bleakness of winter. She wished time would stand still, just for a while, so that she didn't have to grow old, so that things didn't have to change. *Time and tide wait for no man,* she thought wistfully, taking a certain satisfaction from her knowledge of Chaucer.

The four players on the lawn below were having a lovely time. Jasper was one of those people who are good at everything, like his mother, Flappy thought proudly. He had a gift. Whatever he put his hand to, whether it was ball games, skiing, skateboarding, or even cooking, Jasper was a natural. Besides his good looks (another blessing bestowed on him via his mother's exceptional genes), he was affable and charming, charismatic and funny – in fact, Flappy thought as she watched him tap his ball through the hoop, he had it all. All but a job! And, while a job might not have been at the top of Jasper's 'to do' list, it was most certainly a growing concern of Flappy's because for how much longer could she claim to her friends that he was planning on doing something remarkable? For how much longer could she claim he was on the brink of revealing something exciting? For how much longer could she *lie*?

If there was one thing Flappy abhorred, it was lying. But loss of face was something she abhorred even more.

Flappy observed Jasper and Molly, but there was nothing in their demeanour to suggest anything covert or underhand. The four of them chatted and laughed while they moved slowly around the lawn and, even when Jim and Briony's backs were turned, Jasper and Molly behaved as married people should. There was no evidence that they were having an affair. None at all. Yet Flappy could not shake off the feeling that something was being hidden. After all, she had seen Molly cup Jasper's face and gaze dewy-eyed into it. That look was branded on her memory and it still smarted. When Flappy was having her affair with Charles, she had been a master at dissembling. Perhaps Jasper had inherited that from her as well. When all was said and done, the questions remained. What had Jasper been doing at Molly's house and what had they been discussing so secretively at the jumble sale?

Flappy was determined to find out.

Flappy's number one secret agent was Andy Pritchett. Andy didn't know he was a secret agent, which meant that he was all the more secret. Flappy was only too keen now for Molly to use him as much as she wanted, and, it appeared, Andy was only too keen to be used. Flappy assumed he enjoyed transforming their pitiful garden into a thing of beauty. Flappy, more than anyone, understood that, for how the heart sings when it is surrounded by beauty. Nowhere was more beautiful than Darnley, of course, but Hollyberry House had its charm and with Andy working hard in the garden, *that* would acquire some charm too. Flappy's generosity finally reaped its reward when, at the beginning of November, Andy reported, without realizing that he was reporting anything, that Jasper had once again turned up at the house, alone.

Flappy was dismayed. It was all going to go horribly wrong, she was certain. There was no way it wouldn't.

Badley Compton was a small town. Everyone knew each other. It was hard to keep anything secret, unless one was very deft at keeping secrets. However, even Flappy, with all her talents, had been caught. But she had been lucky; would Jasper be lucky too?

There was only one thing to do. She'd have to talk to Jasper, mother to son, and hope that he would be honest with her. The trouble was, it was proving a challenge to get him on his own. He was always doing something with somebody. In typical Jasper style he was making new friends all over Badley Compton and becoming almost as popular as his mother.

Flappy was now meeting Mabel, Sally, Esther and Madge at Big Mary's for coffee two mornings a week at eleven. Flappy was incredibly busy, but she believed it was important to be seen to be mucking in and not remaining in splendid isolation at Darnley. And it was nice, dare she admit it, to be surrounded by her closest friends during this stressful time, for Jasper's lack of work ethic and possible dalliance with Molly Price were, indeed, very worrying. Where would one be, she asked herself, without the support of one's friends? 'Have you finalized the guest list for your party?' Mabel asked. They were seated at their usual table by the window and had ordered coffee and an array of cakes.

'My *ballo in maschera*,' Flappy corrected.

'Yes, that one,' said Mabel.

'I think I have,' Flappy replied.

'You *think* you have?' said Esther, frowning over her coffee cup.

'Well, there are one or two people who are borderline.'

'There are always those,' said Madge.

Sally agreed with a nod. 'You'll end up inviting them in the end because if you don't you'll offend them.'

'That's the trouble,' said Flappy. 'It's hardly worth causing offence for one night, is it?'

'If only one could give a party for the people one likes best,' said Mabel.

Esther gave a throaty laugh. 'Then my party would be very small.'

'Mine too!' agreed Sally.

'The trouble is everyone wants to be invited,' said Flappy with a sigh. 'Sometimes I wonder whether it's worth all the hard work.'

'Oh, it definitely is!' Mabel exclaimed. 'Your parties are always so magical.'

'I know, they are,' said Flappy, 'but one does agonize over the guest list and then the placement. You see, even though I have Persephone, my wonderful Persephone, *I'm* the only person who can take care of the guest list. Who to invite and where to seat them. It's an odious task, really. One is always worried about people being unhappy and I, more than anyone, take such trouble to make sure everyone is happy. It's exhausting.'

'It's going to be such fun, though,' said Mabel. 'When will the invitation land on my doormat?'

'Imminently,' Flappy replied. 'The calligrapher has already

started on the dead-certs.' She smiled at her friends. 'Which means, each of you will get yours first.'

Flappy was feeling light of spirit at the thought of the invitations going out, of people's delight at receiving them – and of the relief of the borderline few. They were rather special, the invitations, being made in the shape of a Venetian palazzo, with a picture of the building superimposed onto the card. It was an inspired idea and one that Flappy would have taken credit for had Persephone not come up with it in front of Kenneth. Well, credit where credit is due, she thought considerately, and she did like Persephone very much. In any case, no one will have ever received an invitation like it, which thrilled Flappy even more because she did like to be the first at everything.

'How's Jasper doing with his new venture?' Sally asked, giving Flappy the electrified look of someone who knows they are soon to be given exciting news.

Flappy reached for her slice of chocolate cake. 'He's very secretive, but I sense it's all going tremendously well.' She took a bite and savoured the sweet taste as it melted on her tongue.

'He's so talented,' said Mabel.

'And so creative,' said Sally.

'I'm sure he'll make a success of whatever he does,' said Madge.

Then Esther, who was always the one brave enough to say what everyone else was thinking, added, 'What *is* it that he does?'

Flappy couldn't speak for her mouth was full, which

was fortunate because now was one of those rare moments when she didn't know what to say. What *could* she say? The four women looked at her expectantly and none of them would have imagined that Flappy was lost for words. They waited patiently while she finished her mouthful and then dabbed her lips with a napkin. 'Well,' she began carefully. 'I don't think it's for me to say. I mean, he's given me the odd glimpse, but I think he wants it to be a tremendous surprise.'

'I love a surprise,' Mabel gushed.

'How like Jasper,' said Madge. 'He's such fun.'

'Yes, he is,' Flappy agreed. 'He's working very hard on plans of some sort, and I'm sure it's going to be thrilling when he makes the big announcement. But what the business is going to be is a mystery.' She took another bite of cake. Now more than ever did she need it. How she hated to lie. How low it made her feel and Flappy, more than anyone, hated feeling low.

'It could be anything, couldn't it?' said Sally thoughtfully. 'I mean, I wouldn't put it past Jasper to announce a publishing deal.' Flappy gave a shallow laugh. What she would give for Jasper to announce a publishing deal!

'Or start a party planning business,' said Mabel.

'Or produce a film,' added Madge, who always ran too far with an idea.

'I don't think it's any of those things,' said Flappy. 'But you're right. He could really put his hand to anything, couldn't he?'

'The main thing is to earn money doing something he loves,' said Esther sensibly. 'Whether it's accountancy or being a personal trainer, it doesn't matter. He just has to enjoy it. Life's too short to do something dull.'

'You're so right, Esther,' said Flappy. 'I don't mind *what* he does, as long as he does *something*,' which wasn't really true. Flappy, more than anything, wanted him to make her proud.

Over the next few days invitations to Flappy's *ballo in maschera* dropped onto the doormats of the fortunate people of Badley Compton who were deemed eligible to receive them. Flappy waited in anticipation for the responses, which she knew would come by return, and for the reactions from her closest friends, which would be full of admiration and wonder. The idea of a masked ball was genius and for that she could take *all* the credit.

The first to call was Mabel, of course. She made it her business to be the first to congratulate Flappy when congratulations were due. She called Flappy at five to nine, knowing that Flappy did not appreciate calls a second before. Wildly excited, her voice trembled as she went through every detail of the invitation, praising Flappy's creativity, style and sheer boldness. 'Only you, Flappy, could do something so unconventional and give it such a sense of class.' Next was Sally, who was thrilled with the Venetian theme and declared she was going to go dressed as an eighteenth-century courtesan. Esther, who followed swiftly after Sally, said she wanted to go as a gondolier, until Flappy told her that the waiters were all going to be dressed as *gondolieri* and that she wouldn't want to be asked by one of the guests to refill their champagne glass.

Madge was late to the telephone as she was late to everything, but equally excited. It was a triumph, obviously.

Briony showed up to swim with Molly and asked Flappy whether the children could come to the party, just at the beginning. 'It would be great for them to see the marquee. They won't have seen anything like it.'

Flappy most certainly did *not* want children at her masked ball. The thought of them tearing about, knocking over displays and putting their greasy fingers on the chair covers make her shiver. However, they *were* her grandchildren so perhaps, just this once, she would allow it. 'Well,' she said thoughtfully, making space in her busy mind for an idea to present itself. 'Maybe just for a little while.' Then, to her satisfaction, an idea popped into her head, and it was truly inspired. 'They can come as street urchins and be part of the theatre,' she declared happily. 'My *ballo in maschera* is, after all, going to be a brilliant piece of theatre.' She envisaged the little rascals in caps and rags, delighting her guests, and felt a touch warmer towards them.

'And Molly's children?' Briony added.

So typical of Briony to ask, Flappy thought. She was beginning to realize that if one gave Briony an inch, she could be relied upon to take a mile.

Molly clapped her hands. 'Wouldn't that be fun! All of them together, like *Oliver Twist's* pickpockets.'

'Jasper can come as Fagin,' Briony laughed.

Flappy was not impressed. Her *ballo in maschera* was going to be authentically Venetian. 'Dickens' *Oliver Twist* was based in London,' she said, drawing on her deep reserves of patience. It was, after all, important to be patient with those less cultivated than oneself. 'Try to find a Venetian equivalent, please,' she told them.

'Of course,' said Molly.

Briony laughed as if she thought Flappy was joking.

'And don't tell anyone else,' Flappy added. 'I don't want hordes of marauding rascals at the party.'

Flappy was finding it difficult to get her son on his own, so it came as a wonderful surprise when Jasper telephoned to invite her out to dinner in town. Not at the golf club where she always went with Kenneth, but somewhere new, somewhere she hadn't been before. Flappy enjoyed restaurants, most of all she enjoyed London restaurants like Le Caprice and The Ritz, where the service and food were of the highest quality. However, when it came to provincial restaurants, Flappy was a highly critical guest. She couldn't help it. She just had very high standards and knew how she liked things done – how things *ought* to be done. If there was one thing Flappy was good at, it was knowing the difference between good taste and bad taste – and there was nothing she abhorred more than tast*eless*. Tast*eless* was a definite no–no, especially when it came to restaurants. However, Jasper did not seem to be concerned, as his father was, about taking his mother somewhere where her critical eye might be offended or displeased. In fact, he found her objections amusing. The table was too close to its neighbour; the food wasn't hot enough; the lights were too bright or too dim; the table wobbled – she unashamedly sent dishes back if they were unsatisfactory or if the milk for her coffee was lukewarm when she had specifically asked for 'piping hot'. His sisters had always cringed with mortification until they had declared, as adults, that they would no longer go to restaurants with her. But Jasper just laughed in his genial way and said that she was absolutely right. When it came to restaurants those things had to be considered. Any restaurateur worth his salt should know that.

It was an overcast evening in early November when Jasper swung by to pick Flappy up in the black Porsche Cayenne Briony had bought (with Kenneth's money). Flappy, in a pair of elegant black trousers, a black Chanel jacket, white silk shirt and her usual gold jewellery, climbed into the passenger seat and immediately commented upon it. 'That wife of yours has very expensive taste,' she said, sweeping her eyes over the high-tech dashboard and glossy leather interior. 'This is more of an aeroplane than a car.'

'Nothing wrong with expensive taste,' Jasper replied pointedly, giving her a knowing smile.

'Nothing wrong with it at all, if one can afford it,' Flappy added tersely.

Jasper laughed. 'Oh ye of little faith.'

'Then give me something to believe in, darling,' she said, hoping he was going to tell her that he had something in mind, that he was busy planning, that tonight was the night he was going to reveal all. But no, he said nothing. They arrived at the quay and Jasper parked the car and escorted her to the little restaurant that overlooked the harbour. It was called The Happy Prawn. Flappy had lived in Badley

Compton for over thirty years and had never set foot in The Happy Prawn. That alone told her that it was either going to be in poor taste or taste*less,* both of which promised an unsatisfactory evening.

However, Jasper pushed open the door and marched in as if he owned the place. He greeted the maître d' with his habitual charm and friendliness and they were given the best table by the window. 'Isn't this great?' he said as they sat down, flicking the napkin onto his knee. Flappy passed her critical eye over the tables and chairs and the bar at the end and decided that the rustic setting was typical of many restaurants all over the West Country. 'It's very cosy,' she said, choosing the least offensive word in the long list of words that sprang to her mind.

'Isn't the location good, though? It looks out over the harbour with all the little boats and is right in the centre of town. Where it all happens.'

'Where the hoi polloi promenade,' Flappy added with a sniff. Flappy preferred settings that were a teeny bit more upmarket.

'I love it,' Jasper stated emphatically. 'In fact, I think it's the nicest place in town.'

'Good,' said Flappy with uninterest. She was much keener to talk about his growing friendship with Molly than waste time discussing the restaurant. Oh for a Wolseley or an Ivy in Badley Compton!

'The food is quite good,' he said, looking down the menu and pulling a face. 'I'd go for the salmon,' he recommended.

'Not the happy prawn?' Flappy asked with a grin.

135

'No, it's not happy. In fact, it's rather glum. I'd definitely avoid the prawn if I were you.'

Jasper chose an expensive wine, which Flappy appreciated. There was nothing she abhorred more than cheap white wine that gave her a headache the following morning. Jasper had the same high standards as his mother and chose a bottle that pleased her. The salmon was also delicious and when the coffee came, the milk was piping hot. However, Flappy was not here for the food, she was here to talk to her son, quite specifically. But she had to be subtle. Jasper was intelligent and sharp. He'd sense the suspicion behind her questions if she didn't gradually work her way up to them. So, she asked him about the children, his games of golf and the people he'd met at the club. They discussed Briony, whether or not she was missing Australia (she was not), and the new friends they were making. It was at that point, during the coffee, which was accompanied by a bowl of chocolate truffles, that Flappy dived in.

'I see you've become very friendly with the Prices,' she said, taking a truffle and popping it into her mouth.

'Yes, they're great,' he replied.

'Has Jim warmed up? I met him at Hedda's for dinner and he was frightfully dull.'

'He's a good bloke, actually, Mum. I think he was unhappy moving here, but he did it for their marriage. For the children. Molly's happy here and now Jim is too. He's set up an office in town and is making good money, which helps.'

'Yes, it does,' Flappy agreed, but she didn't give him a meaningful look. She'd already made her point, countless times. 'You've got close to Molly, haven't you? That's nice. She comes with Briony to use the pool and gym, and my cottage, I might add, which is fine. I'm delighted for them to take pleasure in all the lovely things Darnley has to offer. Andy's been helping her with her garden. He tells me that you pop over every now and then.' She made her tone light and dropped another truffle into her mouth.

'I've been helping Molly with her house,' said Jasper, his tone equally light, but Flappy noticed a faint flush on the apples of his cheeks. A *guilty* flush. He averted his eyes and took a sip of wine.

Flappy stopped chewing. 'With her house?' she mumbled, for her mouth was still full of truffle.

'Yes, it's got lots of potential. With the right advice it could be really something.' Jasper sat back and held her gaze with his now steady one. He was, Flappy knew, making an effort to appear nonchalant.

She frowned. Had she really heard right? 'And you're giving Molly advice?'

'Yes.'

'Since when have *you* been an arbiter of tasteful interior design?'

'I've always loved houses.' He grinned, as if even *he* was aware that the lie was a weak one.

'Really?'

'Oh, Mum, how little you know me.'

Flappy wiped her mouth with a napkin. Jasper wasn't going into interior design, surely? He'd never shown the slightest bit of interest or, it had to be said, good taste. As far as Flappy could tell, Briony took charge of the home, every aspect of it.

'I'm a dark horse,' he said with a laugh. He took the last truffle. 'May I?'

'Of course, I really shouldn't have had the first two.'

'Don't worry, Mum. Dad will still love you a couple of pounds heavier.'

Flappy was horrified. She forgot all about Molly, and Jasper's penchant for interior design, and felt with a sudden twinge of panic the gentle straining of her trousers at the waist. Was it true? Was it possible? Could she have been a teeny bit neglectful recently?

Had she really put on a couple of extra pounds?

Chapter 10

Flappy could not sleep. Kenneth, of course, could. He lay beside her snorting and snuffling as she stared miserably up at the ceiling, worrying about her weight. How *could* she have let it happen? She who was so careful and disciplined and proud of the fact that at her age she still fitted into clothes she'd worn when she was twenty. This was a disaster and so close to her *ballo in maschera* too! Nevertheless, Flappy was not a person to dive under the covers in despair. When there was a crisis, she rose to the occasion like a phoenix out of the ashes, burning with drive and determination to turn something negative into something positive. Indeed, if Flappy was good at one thing, it was solving a problem when a problem needed to be solved. This was one of those moments.

She climbed out of bed and put on her dressing gown. She didn't bother to tiptoe because an earthquake would not have awoken the sleeping pig. Kenneth was immersed in a sea of dreams, eagerly following the little white ball around a fantasy golf course, no doubt. Like a truffle pig, she thought with irritation. It was hard to be gracious when one felt so utterly out of sorts.

She padded down the corridor to a room at the end where she kept, in wall-to-wall wardrobes, clothes she no longer wore. It was an archive of beautiful items which were now out of fashion. Too good to give to charity but no longer relevant to the looks Flappy so mindfully put together. She opened the door and switched on the light. The smell itself made her feel nostalgic. Perfume worn in bygone days reminded her of the Flappy she used to be: young Flappy, student Flappy, sporty Flappy, socialite Flappy. All sorts of Flappys dressed in all sorts of designs. But one trait remained consistently the same: her size; Flappy had always been a trim size ten.

She stood before these clothes as one might stand naked before a freezing cold lake. She knew she had to take the plunge, as unpleasant as it was sure to be. In order to ascertain the full extent of her negligence, she needed to slip into the one item of clothing that had always fitted her like a second skin: her wedding dress. She inhaled through her nostrils, drawing on her inner strength as her guru Murli had taught her to do: in through the nose, out through the mouth, breathing in peace and calm, breathing out negativity. When she was ready, Flappy pulled her nightdress over her head and stood naked in front of the mirrors, which, stuck within the panels of the wardrobe doors, showed her body from every angle. She did not dwell on her reflection, however. It was hard to accurately assess oneself with the eye. One was either too harsh or too lenient. No, the only way to really find out if pounds had been put on where pounds were not welcome was with the tried and tested wedding dress. It never failed.

Gingerly she stepped into it and drew it up over her legs, her thighs, her hips and her waist. Apprehensively, she slipped her arms into the sleeves and then, almost fainting with dread, she slowly pulled up the zip at the side. And here, at this crucial moment, the problem raised its ugly head and could not be ignored or denied. The zip would not be zipped.

Flappy twisted and turned, sucked in her stomach and crossed her legs, but still, the gap between the two sides of fabric refused to close. She had put on more than two pounds, she knew, on her hips, her derrière and her stomach. There was no refuting it. The dress did not lie and, in this unique circumstance where truth to oneself was absolutely paramount, neither did Flappy. She stared at her larger figure with honesty both painful and pure. It was the chocolate cake at Big Mary's and the truffles at The Happy Prawn, among the many other small indulgences she had caved into over the course of the last two months. And all because she'd been anxious. All because of Briony and Jasper and Molly.

She sighed heavily. A sigh laden with frustration and regret. But Flappy was not a woman who was easily defeated. Flappy was a fighter. Right now, she faced a fearsome challenge. But she would rise to it like Jeanne d'Arc, the Maid of Orléans, with her sword held high, her chin proud and her eyes set on her goal. She would get her perfect figure back again, even if it killed her.

A few hours later, Flappy rose, as she always did, at five o'clock. But she did not do yoga, as routine dictated. No, in order to fight those invasive pounds, she needed a more strenuous workout. In the gym were various machines originally bought for Kenneth. Back in the day, Kenneth had been rather trim. He'd used the running machine, the rowing machine and the various other contraptions that had kept him lean. Although it was hard to imagine now, he had, in truth, been lean. Then golf had taken over, along with a certain indolence against which he had fought valiantly with the help of his wife, who had encouraged him to head down to the gym. But Kenneth did not have Flappy's determination and he didn't mind his expanding girth. In fact, he was quite proud of it. It gave him a certain gravitas, he thought, a certain machismo. Being short, the belly added something important. He did not want to do away with it. Now, as Flappy ran on the running machine and felt the sweat pouring down her forehead, she did not think of Kenneth's silhouette. She did not think of Kenneth at all. Her thoughts were entirely of herself. Of her single-minded determination to slip once again into that wedding dress, and to zip it up with one easy, fluid motion.

Flappy spent an hour in the gym. She then went for a swim. The water was pleasantly cool against her hot skin. She did half an hour of lengths. Once she'd tired of front crawl, she did backstroke. When her arms ached, she did breaststroke. And finally, for the last length, she did a kind of doggie paddle-sidestroke because by now she was exhausted and, as no one was watching, she didn't care how she made it to the end. She just needed to get there, without drowning.

With her hair in a towel and her fatigued body wrapped

in a white velour dressing gown, she sat at the island in the kitchen, reading the *Daily Mail* and drinking a cup of hot water and lemon. She wouldn't have breakfast, she decided. Breakfast was calories she didn't need. She'd wait until lunch and then have soup. In fact, hadn't she read, in this very newspaper, that Madonna had once lost weight on a diet of cabbage soup – or was it popcorn? (Popcorn, Flappy thought, was frightfully common.) Soup it would be then, all the way, until those pounds had been shed.

Flappy was not one of those women who pick at food and never feel hungry. She might *look* like she was super-human – many had, indeed, commented on her superhuman traits – but she was a woman with a healthy appetite like any other. However, the difference between Flappy and 'any other' was not simply the gifts of beauty and grace that nature had bestowed upon her, although, to be sure, they played their part, but her strength of mind. Flappy, undeniably, had grit, fortitude and resolve. It was these qualities that set her apart. These qualities that sucked good fortune into the whirlpool of her experience. If Flappy had a charmed life it was not down to luck. It was down to strength of mind. And now, as she decided to skip breakfast and eat only soup *indefinitely*, she applied that exceptional strength of mind. Where others failed, Flappy succeeded. Not a morsel of anything besides soup would pass her lips. Fortunately, Kenneth never noticed what she ate or didn't eat, because he was so focused on his own plate. To Kenneth, food was one of the great pleasures of life along with golf, and both required his absolute attention.

143

When Flappy finished reading the *Daily Mail,* she popped it into the recycling bin and laid Kenneth's place for breakfast. Before putting *The Times* beside his plate she opened it at the leader page and had a quick read, so that she could later comment upon it. She was much too high-minded to base her opinions on a tabloid. Then she went upstairs to dress and blow-dry her hair. Kenneth was still sleeping. He would not stir until nine. Those frantic days of his youth, when the building of his business empire required him to rise before the sun, were long gone. He was a man of leisure now, and deservedly so. Flappy did not resent him for lying in, but she did resent him for occupying her bedroom when she wanted to sit at her dressing table and do her hair. However, she quickly overcame her resentment, for what sort of woman would she be if she begrudged her husband his rest, after everything he had given her? So, with those thoughts of gratitude and consideration, Flappy went into the bathroom where she'd laid out her clothes the night before and got dressed. Then she went to one of the spare rooms to dry her hair. As she sat curling it around a large round brush, she wondered whether she'd be able to coax her husband back into his dressing room. Kenneth was, by all accounts, a tolerant man. If she was clever, she could do it without offending him. If Flappy was one thing, it was clever.

To take her mind off her weight, Flappy went into Chestminster to buy Christmas presents. Being so incredibly busy, she liked to get it done early, preferably in September, but now it was November she really needed to get a move on. Her two daughters, Mathilda and Charlotte, and her youngest son Daniel, who lived in LA, were not spending Christmas with them this year. It was the year they all went to their in-laws. Flappy had arranged it as such so that every *other* year they all got together, somewhere glamorous like the Caribbean.

This year Flappy and Kenneth would have Jasper and Briony and their two children at Darnley. The thought of the children and their dog jumping on her sofas filled her with dread, but envisaging the six of them celebrating around the tree, which was always magnificent, in the hall, which was also magnificent, appeased her somewhat. There would be beautifully wrapped-up presents under the tree, candlelight and music, and Briony would comment on Flappy's good taste and Flappy would thank her, graciously, brushing off her compliments because, really, she was so *so* lucky to have such a lovely house and a lovely family to share it with. It would be an enchanting Christmas, as enchanting as a picture on a Christmas card.

With these thoughts drifting through her mind like happy clouds, Flappy drove into Chestminster. The sky was a crisp blue and seagulls wheeled and glided on the salty wind that swept in off the sea. Autumn had really sunk its teeth into the land, leaving the trees denuded with piles of orange and yellow leaves in puddles at their roots. The air was chillier now, the evenings dark, the mornings blinking sleepily through a thin veil of mist. Yet, the sun was amber gold and Flappy loved the way it settled onto the gardens at Darnley.

Its mellow, peachy light made her think of the good old days when her children were young, when they were together as a family. Just the six of them. Roasting marshmallows on bonfires, collecting conkers and kicking the leaves with their little boots. Those were innocent times. Times that Flappy looked back on with wistfulness and nostalgia. But the children had grown up and flown away, far away, as far away, in fact, as they could possibly have flown, and Flappy sometimes felt sad about that. However, she wasn't going to let regret or self-reflection dampen her mood. It was better, she figured, not to look too hard into the past. Better to appreciate the gloss and not scratch through it to the lacklustre picture beneath.

She parked her Range Rover in the car park and headed to the high street. Chestminster had a very good high street with all the best shops. It was almost as good as strolling up Marylebone High Street, only there was no Selfridges close by, and Flappy did so love Selfridges. Nevertheless, she wandered in and out of the shops, finding things for her grandchildren at Trotters and one or two things for Briony at The White Company. She bought something special for Persephone, because she was, as she had admitted to Hedda, the closest thing to a daughter that Flappy had in Badley Compton. She bought her a cashmere sweater of such beauty Flappy almost decided to keep it for herself.

As she was coming out of a boutique, who should be walking towards her, but Kenneth and Jasper. Flappy stared at them in surprise. What were *they* doing in Chestminster? Why hadn't Kenneth told her they were meeting?

When Kenneth and Jasper saw Flappy, they stared back at her with equal surprise and, Flappy thought suspiciously, guilt.

'Darling,' said Kenneth, putting out his arms as if to embrace her. That in itself was odd. One doesn't embrace one's spouse in the middle of the street.

'Hello, you two. What are you doing here? I thought you were on the golf course. You're always on the golf course.'

'Hi, Mum,' said Jasper, giving Flappy the benefit of his wide and charming smile. It was hard to feel anything other than affection when faced with Jasper's smile.

She looked from one to the other expectantly.

Kenneth's little eyes dropped to the shopping bags she was carrying. 'We're doing what you're doing. Christmas shopping,' he said, but she didn't believe him.

'In November?' she said. Kenneth usually did his Christmas shopping at the last minute and, he had told her himself, he was going to buy her 'something big' this year. Flappy didn't imagine 'something big' could be bought in Chestminster.

'I persuaded him, Mum. There's a piece of jewellery I've got my eye on for Briony.'

'Is there now,' said Flappy, unconvinced. Surely Jasper would head to London for something like that. One didn't find the sort of thing that Briony would expect as a Christmas present here in Chestminster either. And how could he afford it?

'And something I've got my eye on for *you*,' Kenneth added, puffing out his chest and giving his wife a wink.

Flappy turned up her nose. That didn't sound like the 'something big' that he'd mentioned back in September.

'You're as guilty as a pair of schoolboys caught in the grub cupboard. What's going on?'

The two men looked at each other. Jasper sighed. 'If I told you, I'd have to kill you,' he joked.

Flappy pulled a face, the sort of face that demanded the truth.

'Seriously, Mum. It's a surprise. If I tell you, I'll spoil it.'

The thought of a surprise made her heart sink. 'Very well. I hope you're not up to no good.'

Kenneth grinned. 'See you later, then,' he said, and they set off down the street.

Flappy walked on for a block or two, her busy mind whirring with guesses as to what they were *really* doing here. Then she stopped outside an upmarket estate agent. She glanced at the photographs of expensive-looking properties displayed in the window and her heart sank further. Kenneth and Jasper had come from this direction so it was not beyond the realm of possibility for them to have been in here, looking for a house. Well, that would be typical, Flappy thought crossly. Briony was no doubt demanding a place of her own and Kenneth, unable to say no to his son, was going to buy it for them. No wonder they looked so guilty. Kenneth knew very well what she thought about the whole situation. In fact, as she thought about it some more, she felt a craving for the taste of chocolate cake creeping over her skin in a hot flush.

If Kenneth bought them a house, where was the incentive for Jasper to get a job? Flappy's prestige, so hard won in

Badley Compton, demanded that he was gainfully employed. For how much longer could she string her friends along with lies about a big announcement? There was eventually going to come a moment when she'd have to tell them the truth: that Jasper was a man of leisure, living off his father's generosity and his mother's endless patience.

Flappy no longer felt like Christmas shopping. She made her way back towards the car park, feeling low. Where had she gone wrong? Why didn't Jasper have a work ethic like his father? Where was his drive, his ambition, his pride? Both she and Kenneth were people of enterprise and energy. Before Flappy married Kenneth she'd had lots of jobs – admittedly, most of them were not much to shout about: she'd been a shop assistant in the glove department at Harrods, an au pair for a family in Buenos Aires, a receptionist at Claridge's and a chalet girl in Verbier, but the point was that she had worked. She'd had no family money to fall back on. She came from nothing. Jasper and his siblings were raised at Darnley with everything they could ever want. Sure, she had spoiled them because she'd wanted them to enjoy the things she'd never had. Therein lay the mistake, she knew. But spoiling a person didn't entitle them to a life of indolence. After all, Daniel was doing very well. A person with character would always want to make something of their life. Jasper didn't. It was as simple as that.

Flappy found herself standing outside a café, staring at the rows of cakes and buns through the glass. There was something hypnotic about them as if they had voices and were calling to her: *Don't be so hard on yourself. I'll relieve you of your stress. I'll make you feel better. Just a small bite. It won't make the slightest difference.* Flappy tore herself away. Jasper might not have any get-up-and-go, but *she did.*

Persephone was in the kitchen making a cup of coffee when Flappy returned, still feeling dispirited. 'Are you all right, Flappy?' she asked, noticing her boss's taut features and downcast eyes.

Flappy sighed. She knew she could confide in Persephone. 'I bumped into Jasper and Kenneth in town. I thought they were playing golf. They're up to something, those two, I'd bet my life on it.'

'I wouldn't do that,' said Persephone with a smile. 'Coffee?'

'Please.'

'Mr Scott-Booth said they were going Christmas shopping.'

'Did he?'

'Yes, before he left this morning. I didn't know Jasper was going with him, though. Probably looking for something for Briony. She's got expensive taste, that one.'

Flappy sighed again and perched on one of the stools at the island. 'Maybe I'm reading too much into it, Persephone,' she said. 'They just looked very guilty, that's all.'

'Maybe Mr Scott-Booth was buying *you* a present.'

Flappy laughed mirthlessly. 'No, he won't do his Christmas shopping until the last minute and I haven't given him my list yet.'

'How sensible to give him a list.' Persephone brought over her espresso and sat down opposite Flappy.

'I can't trust him to buy me something on his own. He's

many things, is my Kenneth, but he's not the arbiter of good taste. He said he wanted to buy me something big this year. I dread to think what that might be. It's not normal for him to go off-piste, as it were. Without my guidance he might end up spending a lot of money on something I don't want.'

'He's generous, though, which is lovely.'

'He's much *too* generous,' Flappy said drily, thinking of the house he was probably going to buy for Jasper and Briony. She sipped her coffee. It was thick and rich and utterly delicious. 'Enough about me. How's it going with George?'

'Well,' Persephone smiled. 'I think he's going to move down here.'

Flappy was delighted. That was wonderful news. More effective than cake in lifting her out of her blues. 'Has he found a job?'

'He's got an idea. He says he's working on it.'

'What is it?'

Persephone shrugged. 'I don't know. He says he doesn't want to tell me until it's a dead cert.'

'At least he's got an idea. Between you and me, Persephone, I don't think Jasper even *wants* to work. He's showing no signs of looking. I don't even think he has an idea.' Flappy lowered her eyes and took a long, laborious breath. 'I spoiled him. That's the trouble. If only I could turn the clock back . . .'

'You worry too much, Flappy. He's happy. His family are healthy. He's probably the most charming man Badley Compton has ever met. Everyone loves him. So what if his father supports him? How lucky he is to have such a generous dad.'

151

Flappy looked at Persephone with tenderness. 'You're so wise, Persephone. Sometimes I think you were sent to me as a guardian angel, to keep me sane.'

'You want him to be like you, with all your motivation. But he's not like you. He's himself. I think you worry too much. Let him be. He'll probably surprise you one of these days by doing something amazing.'

'Oh, I do hope so.'

'What you *should* be thinking about is what you're going to wear to your *ballo in maschera*.'

'What we're *both* going to wear,' Flappy corrected. 'Have you had any thoughts, Persephone?'

'No, I haven't had the time to think about that.'

'Then let me think about it for you. I suggest we pay a visit to a dressmaker I know who lives a few miles outside Badley Compton. If anyone can create something to turn heads, she can.'

'So far everyone can come,' Persephone said.

'Really? Not one "no"?'

'Not one.'

'Well, that *is* good news. Though, I was rather hoping those borderline people might have a better invitation and decline.'

Persephone laughed. 'That *is* wishful thinking.'

Flappy looked at Persephone, at her wide, honest face, her gentle brown eyes and her sweet smile, and thought how lucky she was to have her. So *so* lucky. 'Thank you for making me feel better,' she said.

'That's what I'm here for,' Persephone replied. 'And, I'm

always here, you know.' And Flappy knew that that phrase, so deliberately spoken, was said to reassure her of her loyalty and discretion. She knew she could count on Persephone.

Flappy drained her coffee cup.

Chapter 11

Twenty minutes later Flappy's shiny grey Range Rover turned into a farm entrance a few miles outside Badley Compton. 'Here we are,' she told Persephone, driving slowly up an avenue of plane trees towards the house. 'I can't wait for you to meet Esmeralda. She's an original,' she added with satisfaction, because Flappy loved people who were out of the ordinary, like her. What she *didn't* like were people who were commonplace. To Flappy's dismay the world was populated by far too many commonplace people, which made them impossible to avoid. But here, in this unlikely corner of Devon, was a woman most extraordinary.

Esmeralda Trott was a lively Mexican septuagenarian, married to an Englishman, living in a run-down farmhouse in the middle of the Devon countryside. Surrounded by fields of cows and rolling pastures, Esmeralda looked out of place, like an exotic orchid in a field of barley. With hair as black as a crow's wing and eyes of emerald green, with her long, colourful skirts and rows of bangles jangling at her wrists, she resembled a gypsy from a fairy tale. Her skill was not in fortune telling, as her attire might suggest, but in sewing, and she sewed exceedingly well. Well enough for Flappy to have discovered her and used her on many occasions when a made-to-measure dress was required. She would have kept her secret, because sometimes it was tiresome being copied, but the Trotts were not well off – farming did not make a man rich, neither did dressmaking – and Flappy, who liked Esmeralda for her warmth and her exuberance as well as her skilled fingers, felt duty-bound to promote her. Flappy was, contrary to what she might say, well aware of the power of her endorsement. One word from her and the women of Badley Compton were sure to follow her lead, as eager sheep to the shepherd's command. Hence Flappy, unselfishly, had spread the word and Esmeralda had been inundated with orders. More orders than she could cope with. Esmeralda was truly grateful and now, as Flappy and Persephone were shown into her messy workroom, she told Flappy that, as a measure of her gratitude, she would not only give her a discount but make her the most beautiful dress she had ever seen. Flappy didn't doubt it.

Esmeralda's workroom was an Aladdin's cave of wonders. Every wall was covered with fabric swatches, designs, photographs, newspaper articles and letters. On the floor were piles of magazines, rolls of fabric and trimmings. There were shelves of books, boxes of buttons and lace, and everywhere one looked something twinkled and caught the eye. In the middle of it all a large, ornamental bird cage hung suspended from the ceiling from where a brightly coloured parrot watched them from his perch. Flappy did not like birds in cages. 'That parrot should be flying over the Amazon rainforest,' she told Esmeralda, but the woman just laughed and shook her head, so that her chunky earrings clinked at her neck.

'He would miss me too much,' she replied in her thick Mexican accent, slipping her finger through the bars for the bird to hold with its beak. 'You see, he says, "Please don't send me away. I don't want the blue skies. I want to be here with you."'

Flappy laughed. 'Poor thing has probably never seen blue sky, only your ceiling.'

'He's very beautiful,' said Persephone. 'What's his name?'

'Lorito.'

'Little parrot.'

'Yes, but he's not so little, eh.' Esmeralda pulled a face. 'He's a greedy parrot. Never satisfied. I tell you, if I put him in a sack of feed he'd eat himself to death.'

Flappy cleared a space on the sofa and she and Persephone sat down. Esmeralda brought over a tray of herbal tea. It tasted of fennel. Then she pulled up a chair, placed a notebook on her knee and looked attentively at the two women. 'Tell me, what do you want me to make for you?'

Flappy explained the concept of her *ballo in maschera*, which Esmeralda immediately understood. 'What a marvellous idea,' she exclaimed, her eyes sparkling at the thought of such a wonderful challenge.

'I wanted to do something original, something different,' said Flappy, pleased that Esmeralda appreciated the genius of the idea. 'Something that Badley Compton has never seen before.'

'They will have never seen a masked ball,' said Esmeralda.

'Persephone and I want to stand out, don't we, Persephone?' said Flappy. 'We want to look like eighteenth-century ladies in big, beautiful dresses and flamboyant masks.'

'*Grand* ladies,' added Esmeralda with emphasis. 'Princesses.'

'Queen,' Flappy corrected.

'Flappy must be the queen of the ball,' Persephone agreed. 'I'd like my dress to be a little more "discreet princess". If you don't mind, Flappy.'

Flappy was delighted. There was, after all, only one hostess and it was customary for her, indeed it was expected of her, to shine the brightest of all the pretty things at the ball. Besides, it wasn't in Persephone's nature to draw attention to herself. Flappy, on the other hand, loved nothing more than drawing the eye when she was prepared and ready for it to be drawn. Her *ballo in maschera* would be one of those occasions when she would radiate more intensely on account of hours of groundwork, and it all started here, with the dress.

After a long discussion and another pot of tea, Esmeralda drew some sketches. She was a good drawer – Flappy looked like Flappy and Persephone looked like Persephone, and it quickly became apparent that Esmeralda knew very well what shape suited which woman best. 'I suggest silvers and golds for you, Flappy, and blues and greens for you, Persephone,' said Esmeralda. 'And I will make you the most lavish masks,' she added with a grin. 'You know, a lot of naughtiness goes on at these balls.'

Flappy laughed nervously. She could already visualize

157

Charles trying to entice her into a clinch. How very close they had come to kissing in the pool house . . .

'But that is why you have chosen the theme, of course,' Esmeralda continued. 'It is an opportunity for people to behave badly, no?'

'Oh, I don't think so,' said Flappy, doubting that anyone (except for Charles) would have the nerve to behave badly at Darnley.

'I think Badley Compton is much too quiet for that,' said Persephone.

But Esmeralda was not put off. 'It's the quiet ones you need to watch out for,' she laughed. Once she had finished, she put down her sketchbook. 'I presume your husband needs a costume?'

Flappy had been so busy thinking about herself that she'd forgotten all about Kenneth. 'Yes, I suppose he does,' she said vaguely.

'Then I will design him an outfit that complements yours,' said Esmeralda. 'And you?' She turned to Persephone. 'Do you have a husband?'

Persephone blushed. 'No, I have a boyfriend, but he's doing his own thing.'

'When he sees you in my creation he will want to marry you at once, if only to stop anyone else from having you.'

Persephone's blush deepened. 'It's much too early for that,' she laughed.

Flappy and Persephone left the farmhouse in high spirits, confident that they were going to look every inch Venetian ladies. Flappy was confident that she would look every inch more fabulous than everyone else. As the Range Rover turned out into the lane, who should be turning in, but Hedda. Flappy rolled down her window. 'Hedda! What a surprise.'

'I'm coming to have a dress made for your ball,' said Hedda. 'Big Mary told me that Esmeralda Trott is the best dressmaker outside London.'

'Yes, my words exactly,' said Flappy. She wasn't sure whether to be pleased or put out that her friend was having a dress made by the same dressmaker. Then she was struck by a horrible thought. Perhaps *all* the ladies of Badley Compton were going to come here in droves. Flappy wondered whether she should put out a statement forbidding anyone to have a dress made in silver and gold. But then she reassured herself that Esmeralda would not make anything for anyone else that even remotely resembled hers.

'I'm so excited, Flappy. The invitation is stunning. It requires a stunning costume,' Hedda continued.

'Well, you're coming to the right place,' said Flappy. Then, unable to resist, she added, 'Try not to tell anyone else about Esmeralda. Let's keep her a secret between the two of us.'

'I don't think you need to worry, Flappy. Big Mary told me that no one else can afford her. Apparently, since you promoted her, she's put up her prices.'

Flappy felt better now that Hedda had acknowledged that Esmeralda was *her* find and not Big Mary's. 'Well, that's a very good thing,' she said. And, even though Flappy had put on a few extra pounds, there was no way that Hedda, being her size and shape, would outshine her. There was only room for one queen at the ball and Flappy was satisfied that it would be *her*.

December blew in with gales and snow. It was unusually cold. The coldest it had been in one hundred years. Flappy lit fires in all the rooms that had fireplaces and turned up the heating. If there was one thing she hated, it was being cold. However, the gardens did look magical in the hard winter sunshine. Like an Advent calendar, all white and twinkly, as if the world had been sprinkled with glitter. In fact, as she stood at the window and gazed out over the gardens, Flappy didn't think there was anywhere in England more beautiful than Darnley in the snow. It was flawless and smooth, like a wedding cake.

Flappy's grandsons, who had never seen snow before, were wildly excited, building snowmen all over the croquet lawn with carrots and coal and making a terrible mess of the immaculate white quilt that had covered the grass. They stood with their mouths open, catching the flakes and laughing as they melted on their tongues. School had broken up and it seemed to Flappy that Kim and the children spent more time at Darnley than they did in their own house. Not that she minded. What sort of woman would she be if she failed to take pleasure from little people enjoying the fabulous facilities and space of her home? No, Flappy was delighted that they ruined the splendour of her lawns, splashed about in the swimming pool, jumped all over Kenneth's exercise machines and pressed their snotty noses and wet mouths against the glass, leaving smudges for her to wipe when she came down in the mornings to work out. Perhaps 'delighted' wasn't entirely accurate, but that is what she told Mabel and the ladies when they met at Big Mary's. 'I'm so *so* lucky to see so much of my grandchildren,' she said and then, envisaging the marred perfection of her lawns, only just managed to resist the cake.

It wasn't just Tom and Jack, but Buster too. The dog also tore about the lawns, rolling in the snow, leaving pawprints in ever increasing circles. Then the Price children came as well, with Molly, who didn't have an au pair, followed unsurprisingly by Jasper, and finally Kenneth who, unable to play golf, made the children an igloo and taught them how to sledge down the slope on trays. However, it continued to snow and soon the pawprints and footprints were covered in a fresh layer of perfection and Flappy could once again look out of the window and take pleasure.

She was still going to the salon for a blow-dry twice a week, even though she was now having to do her own hair every other day on account of her new swimming and workout regime. It was time she relished. An hour to sit and read magazines which were beneath her dignity to buy, like *Hello!*, and to catch up on news of the famous personalities that interested her. Flappy turned up her nose at celebrities, mostly because she didn't know who any of them were. Footballers' wives (Flappy wasn't in the least interested in football), reality show stars (Flappy did *not* watch reality TV under any circumstance) and minor actors (Flappy was only interested in the properly famous ones). She enjoyed reading about royalty, because they were royalty, and dukes and duchesses, lords and ladies and other members of that rarefied, inaccessible club to which she would never belong. She liked reading about them a lot, but she would never *ever* allow such magazines to cross the threshold of Darnley, which was, it must be emphasized, an establishment of culture and good taste. No, the only place in which Flappy permitted herself to indulge in that kind of reading matter was at the hair salon. Even Lady Micklethwaite, when she had lived at Compton Court, had been seen flicking through *Hello!* while her hair was wrapped in foil.

One morning, when the hour was up and Flappy left the salon with hair that caused the turning of many a head on the high street, she decided to go to the deli to buy something for Kenneth's supper. She was going to Hedda's for bridge and dinner, leaving Kenneth to dine at home alone. Kenneth never minded being left on his own. He liked to eat his supper in front of the television and watch programmes that didn't interest Flappy, like game shows and sport. Even though he wasn't able to play golf in the snow, he still went to the club every day for lunch, so he did not require anything too substantial for supper. Smoked salmon on toast would do, or a small steak and kidney pie from the deli.

As she approached the deli, Flappy noticed a man walking in front of her in a black beanie hat and black coat. His hands were stuffed into his pockets, but he had a lively walk and a whistle upon his lips. A merry whistle. The whistle of a someone who has no cares. It made Flappy smile to watch him. How she envied him, this man with no cares, for she was riddled with them and she wasn't even allowed to comfort herself with cake. The diet was going well, of course, because Flappy stuck to it as a nun to her vows, but it wasn't easy, living such a stressful life and not being able to find solace in carbohydrates.

Soon the man turned into the deli. Flappy followed. She was curious to see more of this cheerful creature. The door closed behind her, tinkling a little bell, and the salty aroma of fine food assaulted her nostrils. The man turned and to her surprise Flappy saw the almost unrecognizable face of Jim Price. No longer the blank, dull countenance of a man dogged by depression but the pink, animated face of a man released from his troubles. 'Jim!' she exclaimed.

'Flappy,' he replied with equal surprise.

'Are you well?' Flappy realized that that was a silly question, for he was obviously exceedingly well.

'Yes, I'm enjoying Badley Compton more than I ever thought I would.'

Well, that was almost more words than he had said all evening at Hedda's dinner party. 'How wonderful!' Flappy exclaimed. 'It is a special place, isn't it?'

Jim smiled and Flappy was taken aback by how attractive he was when animated. Who'd have thought it? Really, he should smile more often. 'I managed to find an office with a view of the harbour,' he continued, 'and have been inspired. I had a terrible block in London, but down here my creative juices are flowing. I've never been so inspired. It's great.'

'The people here are good, wholesome people,' said Flappy in the tone of a queen praising her subjects. 'Their hearts are in the right place. They have the right values. London is all very well, but I imagine, for a creative person, it's hard to find the space to create. The space in one's mind, of course. It's all so busy and frantic.'

'You're right,' Jim agreed. 'Molly and I have met some very nice people. Jasper and Briony to name but two. We're lucky they chose to move here at the same time we did.'

'Yes,' said Flappy, trying not to show her unease. She didn't imagine that he knew how often Jasper visited his wife. The thought of it made Flappy grow hot under the collar. She put a hand to her throat. 'Living in a lovely place is all very well, but it's the people that make it. I'm so pleased you've met some like-minded folk.'

Jim smiled again and Flappy frowned. It was hard to reconcile the bloodless man she'd first seen in her seat in church with the rudely healthy man who was grinning at her now. They were like two entirely different people. Flappy knew nothing about depression, but if Jim was anything to go by, she realized what a shadow of oneself it made one into.

Flappy bought Kenneth a steak and kidney pie and headed home feeling more anxious than ever about Jasper's erring ways.

That evening, while Kenneth sat in his favourite armchair, watching what Flappy considered a very tacky game show and tucking into his pie and a large glass of Merlot, Flappy drove to Compton Court. She sang along to ABBA's 'The Winner Takes It All', which was one of her favourite songs and her secret weapon when, as a young woman, she'd gone to karaoke parties. Really, there hadn't been a dry eye in the room when she'd belted out the chorus. Pitch perfect, voice quivering ever so slightly, a hint of a Swedish accent to give the song an authentic ring. Now she sang it to herself in the car and figured that, even though she was older, her voice was still as good as it ever was. Perhaps she'd host a karaoke party at Darnley and ask the guests to come in fancy dress. As she motored through the grand gates of Compton Court she envisaged herself in an electric-blue jumpsuit and platform boots. Once she'd lost weight she thought she'd pull off the look most beautifully.

To her surprise, Charles met her at the door. 'How lovely you look tonight, Beauty,' he said, gazing at her longingly. Flappy wondered where Johnson was, for usually he saw to the door and escorted her into the drawing room. She rather loved the fact that they had a butler. It was wonderfully grand and Flappy did love grand, although she was slightly jealous that she didn't have a butler at Darnley.

'Charles,' she said, caught off guard. She hadn't expected to see him. Normally, he wasn't around for Hedda's bridge nights.

'I had to see you,' he said with an urgency that alarmed her.

'Why? What's happened?'

'*You've* happened, Flappy.'

Flappy sighed. Well, if that was all . . .

'You've got under my skin and I can't think of anything else but *you*.' At least he hadn't noticed that she'd put on weight, she thought as she stood on the step, waiting for him to stand aside to let her pass. 'I'm a fool,' he groaned. 'I was reckless. If it wasn't for my recklessness we'd still be meeting in that cottage of yours and—'

'It was wrong, Charles,' Flappy interrupted, before he articulated exactly what they'd got up to and caused her to blush. 'I was a fool for allowing it to happen.' Oh, how she longed for it to happen again.

'And you befriended my wife.'

'I couldn't help that.'

'Pity.'

Flappy inhaled the familiar scent of his cologne and suffered a moment's dizziness. She put a hand on the door frame. 'Charles, we cannot have everything we want in life. Of course, I would love nothing more than to be happily married to Kenneth and, at the same time, enjoy spending time with you.' That was politely put, she thought with satisfaction. 'But it's not possible. We both made our marriage vows and we must stick to them. We're lucky Hedda was so good about it. I know Kenneth wouldn't be. I'm not dancing so close to the flames again.' *Oh, but just one more time . . .*

Charles let out a long sigh which was more of a groan. 'And how you dance.' Suddenly, he grabbed her round the waist and pulled her into his arms, pressing his mouth to her lips in an ardent kiss. Flappy, for a second, forgot herself. Her lips parted. Her eyes closed. Once more they were under

166

the eaves in the cottage. He was her Beastie and she was his Beauty. She invited him in and Charles, with the passion of one of Charity Chance's heroes, kissed her deeply. It was a sensual and voluptuous kiss, one of his finest, but Flappy, deep down in the place where right and wrong are calibrated, knew it was wicked.

She shook her head and swiftly came to her senses.

With a monumental force of will she managed to push herself away and wriggle out of his arms. 'We mustn't, Charles,' she whispered, feeling her heartbeat thumping against her ribcage.

'It's useless fighting against something so powerful, Beauty. We are left no choice but to surrender to it.'

'We must try or we risk losing everything. Our families, our homes, our friends, *everything.*'

This seemed to have a sobering effect, as if she had thrown a bucket of cold water over Charles's head. 'You're right,' he conceded softly after a long pause. 'We must control ourselves and be grateful. At least we can see each other.' He smiled and Flappy thought she might swoon. His smile was, although she barely dared admit it, even to herself, a powerful aphrodisiac. 'Come, I'd better escort you into the drawing room. Hedda will be wondering what we're doing.' And with that he stepped aside to allow her to enter the hall. She slipped out of her coat and he hung it up in the cupboard. 'Where's Johnson?' she asked, collecting herself.

'Serving drinks. I told him *I* would answer the door.'

'Oh, Charles,' she said, giving him a tender smile.

'I just wanted to have a moment with you alone.'

'Oh, Charles,' she repeated, because the look in his eyes was so helpless it caused something inside her heart to snag.

'You're one of a kind, you know,' he said.

And Flappy knew that he was right.

Chapter 12

Flappy was losing weight. Yes, she was denying herself all the things that gave her pleasure, like yogurt, bananas, raisins, milk, wine and, obviously, cake, but she knew that the real reason she was losing weight was because of the nervous energy expended on Jasper. And Jasper, carefree and nonchalant, had no idea of the stress he was causing his mother. He went about his day, pleasing himself in the same way that his father did, only Kenneth had earned his leisure. Jasper had not.

In the old days Flappy could micromanage her children's lives and she had, most efficiently. They were pushed to excel at school and, although they complained bitterly, they complied, because Flappy could be quite terrifying when disobeyed. Kenneth encouraged them to enjoy themselves, to find things they loved doing, whatever that might be, and not to put so much emphasis on academic achievement. After all, *he* had left school at sixteen without any qualifications and look what a success *he* had made. Flappy disagreed. Kenneth had an unusually driven nature, she claimed. Thousands of children came out of school with little to show for it and made nothing of their lives. She wasn't going to allow her children to embarrass her. It was thanks to Flappy that Jasper and Daniel had gone to Cambridge, Charlotte had gone to Edinburgh and Mathilda to Oxford, and they had all, every one of them, attained excellent degrees. Flappy wasn't a woman to boast. In fact the one thing she most abhorred were parents who crowed about their children's achievements. But she couldn't deny that she had taken great pleasure from allowing it to be known, subtly and seemingly without contrivance, just what high achievers her children were. However, they had grown up and left home and Flappy had lost control. It was that lack of control that irked her most about Jasper. She was certain he was having an affair with Molly (and she was always right). But she was powerless to do anything about it.

However, she had lost weight and that was a triumph.

Flappy turned her attention to Christmas and her *ballo in maschera*. The snow had melted and Kenneth and Jasper were back on the golf course, but Flappy managed to get them to buy her a massive Christmas tree and put it up in the hall. Every year, Flappy's tree was revealed at the Christmas drinks she hosted on 23rd December (and a week earlier when, every other year, she, Kenneth and the rest of the family spent Christmas in the Caribbean). It was a fixed event in the Badley Compton social calendar, not unlike the switching on of the Oxford Street Christmas lights in London. The locals gathered in the hall and spilled onto the forecourt to witness the big moment when the local grandee, Lady Micklethwaite last year, Hedda this year, flicked the switch and the tree was revealed in all its magnificence, because the tree at Darnley was, undeniably, magnificent.

Flappy took great trouble with its decorating, planning months in advance what theme she was going to choose and then heading to London to buy what was required. No expense was spared. This year Flappy took Persephone with her. They stayed the night at Claridge's, which was Flappy's favourite hotel, and dined at The River Café. They shopped all day in the crisp winter sunshine, pausing only for a quick lunch at Le Caprice, where Jesús, the handsome Bolivian maître d', who was almost more famous than the restaurant, gave Flappy a warm welcome and the best table in the corner by the window. Flappy, in a chic Prince of Wales check trouser suit and crisp white shirt, cut quite a dash and turned every head in the room. She noticed, with delight, that many of those heads belonged to the glamorous people she read about in *Hello!* magazine. How she loved coming to London and being *seen*.

The theme for this year's Christmas tree was nostalgia; the colours, gold with a touch of crimson. Flappy and Persephone headed straight to Harrods where they found almost everything they needed. Flappy adored Harrods. She'd worked there in her youth and watched with envy the grand ladies, dressed in beautiful clothes and fine jewellery, sweeping through the departments buying whatever took their fancy without even looking at the prices. In those days

Flappy had barely had two coins to rub together, was living in a rented flat with a girlfriend in Hackney and bought her clothes from second-hand shops, although, by the stylish way she threw things together, no one would ever have known they were not couture. All she'd had was her beauty and her intelligence, which, clearly, were of a very superior quality and destined to lift her above the pitiful circumstances of her birth and propel her into the high society she craved. She had become one of those elegant women she had envied from behind the counter in the glove department, being fawned over by staff, smiled at by other like-minded shoppers, and swanning about filling the basket Persephone carried with baubles and tinsel, as much as she wanted, without even glancing at the price tags. Harrods made Flappy forget her present worries and transported her back to a time when she had different struggles. It felt good to reflect on how far she had come. Life is what one makes it, she thought as she thanked the doorman with a smile, stepping onto the pavement, and she had made a great success of hers.

Before taking the train back to Devon, Flappy took Persephone up the Portobello Road. There, she knew, she'd find baubles to fulfil the nostalgic part of her theme. They buzzed from stall to stall, shop to shop, like a pair of bees high on nectar. They chatted to the locals, stopped for a coffee in a café and filled bags with decorations from a bygone era when the streets were cobbled and the only way to travel was on horseback or in a carriage. Flappy was very pleased with her purchases. The tree was going to be beautiful and everyone would admire it as one of her finest. It was always a challenge to try to better the one from the year before, but somehow Flappy managed not to disappoint. If there was one thing Flappy abhorred, it was disappointing people.

The children, the *four* children, because Flappy's grandsons were inseparable from the Price children, were wildly excited about the Christmas tree. They'd never seen one so tall, indeed its highest branch almost touched the ceiling, and the ceilings were very high at Darnley. Briony immediately suggested that the children help decorate it. This suggestion, so innocently made, was a faux pas, because everyone knew that the project was Flappy's and Flappy's alone. Persephone was permitted to assist, but following Flappy's detailed instructions to the letter. There was no room for error. Much rested on the tree – Flappy's reputation as the most stylish woman in Badley Compton to mention but one important factor; the status of Darnley Manor as the focal point of the town to mention but another. The tree was Flappy's way of asserting her superiority while at the same time demonstrating her generosity with the fine mulled wine and mince pies (Big Mary's) that she offered to those who came to celebrate. Darnley was, Flappy knew, like the star of Bethlehem, leading the good people of Badley Compton to witness the magnificent tree, a symbol of Christmas, and to come together in celebration of Christ's birth. It was her duty as a Christian and, of course, as the unofficial but very much accepted queen of the town, to unite the flock at this very special time. It was *not* a time for Briony and Molly's children to make a mess of the tree.

'How many years have you decorated the tree on your

own?' Briony asked Flappy at the family lunch Flappy had arranged on the last Sunday before Christmas.

Flappy did not like the direction this conversation was taking. Kenneth, who knew very well what the tree meant to his wife, did nothing to deflect it. He and Jasper sat tucking into their roast beef and Yorkshire puddings which Karen had cooked, listening with uninterest, while the two young boys ate their food in silence, hoping they might be allowed to play with the decorations that Flappy had laid out on the billiard table in the games room. If Flappy had her way, they would not.

'I've always decorated the tree on my own. It's tradition,' said Flappy.

That might have ended the conversation, but Briony was not a woman to let something go when she felt strongly about it. 'The decorating of the tree should surely be a family event,' she insisted. 'That's the whole point of Christmas, isn't it?'

Flappy was dismayed that after a few months in England, Briony's Australian accent was undiminished. 'Don't you have a tree in your house?' Flappy asked.

'It's a small one. There isn't enough room for a proper one.'

'Aren't the children going to decorate it?'

'Yes, but it's not the same as yours. Yours is amazing. I mean, you've got the perfect house for a really massive tree. It would be fun to decorate it all together.'

'It would be fun,' Flappy agreed with a tight smile. 'But tradition is tradition, after all.'

Briony laughed in that coarse way of hers that made

Flappy feel a little uncertain. She never quite knew whether her daughter-in-law was laughing with her or at her. 'But you're the one who's made the tradition. Surely you can *un*make it?'

'Of course I could. But the town expects certain standards here at Darnley.'

'I think they expect you to lead by example. What sort of an example will you be sending out if your own grand-children are prevented from decorating the Christmas tree? You might be the second most important person in Badley Compton, but you're also a grandmother.' Briony wasn't giving up.

Flappy was put out. She knew that Hedda was the niece of a marquess, but Hedda had only lived in Badley Compton since August. Flappy had lived there for thirty years. When it came to importance, Flappy considered herself the clear winner.

'Kenneth darling, will you pass the water,' she said, hoping to break the conversation and invite the others to talk about something else. 'Is that good, Jack? Are you enjoying your beef, Tom?'

'I want to decorate the tree,' said Tom, pushing out his lower lip.

'Me too,' agreed Jack. Two protruding lower lips faced Flappy. What sort of woman would she be if she ignored them?

'The trouble is, Mum, they consider Darnley home,' said Jasper.

'Yes,' rejoined Briony. 'Our cottage is only rented so it's

not ours, whereas their dad grew up here. This is his home. It'll always be his home. And he's told the kids—'

'Children,' Flappy corrected.

Briony inhaled through her nostrils. '*Children*,' she repeated with forced patience. 'About when he was a little boy, it was a special event to decorate the tree with his brother and sisters. Kenneth arranged a treasure hunt in the garden and whoever won was allowed to put the star on the top.'

Jasper smiled with nostalgia. 'Do you remember, Mum, that time Daniel snuck down in the middle of the night and ate all the chocolates?'

'Yes, I do. The following year I had to make sure they were hung out of reach of his little hands.'

'And we all made our own Father Christmases and reindeers with card and cotton wool and shiny paper, and hung them alongside your expensive glittery balls. It was rather magical, wasn't it?'

'And your father would put up the lights. He was always good at doing that.'

'We'd listen to Cliff Richard singing carols,' said Kenneth with a chortle, refilling his glass with claret.

'The fire would roar in the grate and my scented candles would fill the air with cinnamon. Yes, they were happy times.' Flappy was beginning to feel a little sad. 'Mathilda and Charlotte would make mince pies. Oh, the mess they made of the kitchen. Daniel would insist on watching *The Wizard of Oz*, which was always on the TV over Christmas, and you, Jasper, would make us all play board games after dinner.'

'Or charades,' said Jasper.

'I was rather good at charades,' Flappy recalled, her cheeks now flushed with nostalgia.

'Yes, you were, darling,' Kenneth agreed. 'And karaoke. You sang "The Winner Takes It All" beautifully. Not a dry eye in the house.'

'Oh, Kenneth,' Flappy sighed, feeling a tightness in her chest. 'Weren't those fun times?'

'Fun times don't have to be exclusively in the past,' said Briony. 'They can be now. We can play Cliff Richard, light the fire and candles, and decorate the tree all together. The children have made their own decorations, haven't you, boys?' The two children nodded and gazed at Flappy with sad-dog eyes. 'They'd love to put them up on your tree. They'd be so proud.'

Flappy sensed she was going to have to back down. After all, what sort of grandmother would she be if she denied her grandchildren the fun of a full and proper Christmas? The tree was the central part of the festival, and Christmas was, as Briony had so rightly said, a family event. Flappy put her knife and fork together on her plate and wiped the corners of her mouth with a napkin. An ugly image of a crowd of disappointed townspeople greeting the presentation of a tree covered with home-made bric-a-brac appeared and swiftly disappeared in her mind. What did it matter? she told herself. Family must come first.

'Very well,' she said, turning to the children. 'You can decorate the tree.'

Jack and Tom broke into a noisy cheer.

'But,' Flappy continued. 'We will do it together, slowly and carefully, and you must do as I say.'

'We will, Grandma,' said Jack. Tom nodded because his mouth was full of potato.

'Thank you, Flappy,' said Briony, beaming a glossy smile. 'You're amazing. You really are. You know, I think one of the best things about you is that you're always ready to listen and change your mind. So many people are too proud to back down, but not you.'

'I agree,' said Kenneth. 'Flappy always puts others before herself.'

'Shall we make a toast to Mum,' said Jasper.

'Oh, really, darling,' said Flappy, suddenly feeling very good about her U-turn. 'You don't have to do that. I'm very happy to admit when I might do things a little better.'

'No, I want to,' Jasper insisted. He raised his glass. 'To Mum and all the many things you do for us.'

Kenneth, Briony and the boys raised their glasses too. 'To Grandma,' they said.

Flappy blushed and her eyes sparkled and she realized that she was so *so* lucky to be appreciated, because how many of the thoughtful little things that she did for other people on a daily basis went unnoticed? She smiled at her family with gratitude.

'And I raise my glass to *you*,' she said, lifting her tumbler of water into the air. 'Because you inspire me to be the best wife, mother, mother-in-law and grandmother that I can possibly be.'

Flappy decided that, if she was going to allow the children to help decorate the tree, then she might as well go the whole hog and give them free rein. It was either a Flappy tree or a family tree; it couldn't be a hybrid. The people of Badley Compton needed to be in no doubt as to what kind of tree it was. And so it was, on a grey rainy day, that Cliff Richard was played on Kenneth's old gramophone, the fire was lit in the hall, scented candles gave off the festive smell of Christmas and Kenneth, Flappy, Jasper, Briony, Tom and Jack adorned the tree with all the gorgeous things Flappy had purchased in London, but also with the sweet home-made decorations that the children had crafted themselves. Persephone bought mince pies from Big Mary's, which Flappy managed to resist, and made the tea. Flappy found, to her surprise, that she had more pleasure decorating the tree with her family than she would have had on her own. What's more, Briony didn't say 'kids' once and the children didn't put a single sticky finger on her chair covers. At the end of the afternoon the tree looked a mess. A *wonderful* mess. The kind of mess only small children can make. Flappy wasn't sure whether it was a triumph or a disaster and she waited with dread for 23rd December when the locals would, she was in no doubt, let her know.

Over the following few days Flappy was plagued with anxiety. She met the ladies in Big Mary's and everyone was talking about her tree. 'I can't wait to see what you've done this year,' said Big Mary, bringing over Flappy's cup of coffee.

'How's that tree coming along?' asked John Hitchens, Mabel's husband, when he popped in for a takeaway.

'I bet it's even more spectacular than last year,' said Mabel.

'Every year is always more stunning than the last,' said Esther.

'Well,' Flappy replied, 'I've done something very different this time.'

'It's bound to be amazing!' enthused Sally. 'It's always *amazing*.'

Flappy longed to find comfort in a slice of chocolate cake, but she'd done so well in losing weight that she restrained herself. After all, if the tree was a disaster then she'd have to shine all the more brightly at her *ballo in maschera*.

Later, when she stopped off at the deli, she bumped into Joan Willis, the vicar's wife, and even she, the dullest woman in Badley Compton, grew animated when she mentioned Flappy's tree. 'I don't know how you do it, Flappy,' she said, gazing on Flappy with admiration. 'Everything you do has such style. I'm just dying to see what you've done this year. I think the whole town is.'

Even in the street, as she passed a group of acquaintances talking outside the bookshop, Flappy distinctly heard the words: 'Flappy', 'Christmas tree', 'always outstanding'.

The pressure was on. She wasn't sure she could take it. The night before the big reveal she woke up in a cold sweat wondering whether she should sneak downstairs and redo it. The children would be upset, of course, and Briony wouldn't hesitate to show her displeasure, but the townspeople would be impressed. Flappy wasn't sure whether 'family first' had been such a good idea.

She awoke at the usual time and, although groggy with

lack of sleep, headed down to the gym for her yoga session. However, her mind was buzzing with worry, teeming with dark images of angry townspeople brandishing pitchforks and shouting the words, 'vulgar', 'graceless', 'tacky', that she was unable to hold any of the positions, let alone breathe in rhythm. Desperate, suddenly, for some respite, Flappy put on her coat and boots and hurried down the path to the cottage, illuminating her way with a torch.

Inside the cottage it was warm and cosy. She lit the candles and incense and switched off the lights. The Buddha statue glowed an otherworldly green and, in the eerie radiance of the candles, looked as if it were hovering above its base. Flappy settled down on the cushions, took up the Lotus position, rested her hands one over the other and closed her eyes. She began to chant. At first her mind was invaded by images, bombarding her attempts at attaining some sort of tranquillity, but then little by little, as her breathing slowed and her heart rate decelerated, she dived like a swimmer into the depths of her unconscious, leaving those torpedoes far behind, like missiles dropped onto the surface of the sea.

It was quiet and still down there. Free from cares and worries. Free from the cravings of the ego and the demands of the self. In fact, Flappy lost sense of the self altogether. Here, she communed with eternity, blended with the source and became one with the great Oneness of which we are all part.

Thanks to Flappy's intense meditation, by the time the sun sank behind the trees and a thin veil of mist fell upon the gardens, she was feeling quite relaxed. Everything was set up for the Christmas drinks. Big Mary's mince pies were in the oven, the mulled wine was ready to serve and a small troop of helpers, led by Persephone, had arrived to wait on the crowd that was about to arrive at any moment.

Flappy was glad to see that Briony had dressed the children appropriately. They wore matching black corduroy trousers, white shirts and red sleeveless V-neck sweaters. Their hair had been brushed and their faces washed and they looked adorable, as if they'd never put a greasy finger mark on a cushion in their lives. Flappy was deeply proud.

Jasper and Briony were a picture of togetherness and Flappy decided that tonight she was not going to worry about Jasper and Molly. She was not going to worry at all. She was going to hold onto that feeling of Oneness that she had felt in her meditation and rise above the petty cares of the mortal world. Tonight was about Christmas, about celebrating the birth of Christ and about following his fine example and sending love and kindness out into the world.

However, when people began to turn up, parking their cars in the field and walking to the house along a path lit by flares, Flappy felt herself being dragged back into those petty cares. She no longer felt at one with the great Oneness, but isolated and alone in her mortality. It was too late to change the tree now. What on earth had she been thinking?

Mabel and John Hitchens were the first to arrive, followed closely by Madge, Sally and their husbands, children and grandchildren, and Esther who wasn't married. Graham and Joan came next, then Hedda, Charles, George and his siblings, and after them, Jim and Molly with their children followed by a constant trickle of locals, all twittering like excited robins, anticipating the revealing of the tree and the switching on of the Christmas lights.

'You don't need to worry,' said Persephone, passing Flappy with a tray of mulled wine in glasses. 'Tonight isn't really about the tree. It's about the community coming together and having a good natter, a few glasses of mulled wine and Big Mary's mince pies.'

Flappy wished she were right. She was not. Tonight was about the tree. *All* about the tree. And this year Flappy was going to deliver a flop.

At last the moment arrived, as moments always do, and Flappy found herself standing on the steps by the front door about to speak to a sea of expectant faces. Her heart fluttered in her chest and her throat went dry. She took a sip of mulled wine and a deep, calming breath. She thought of her Buddha, of Murli, of her family and friends and tried to think of something to say. Just as she was about to speak, Tom and Jack came and sat on the step at her feet. They looked up at her with wide, shiny eyes and pink cheeks and suddenly an idea plopped into Flappy's worried mind.

'My dear friends, tonight is always such a special night. But this year it is even more so, because I'm here with my son Jasper and his wife Briony and my two darling grandchildren, Tom and Jack.' The boys waved and the crowd laughed. 'Every year I invite you all to celebrate Christmas with Kenneth and me and every year I try to make the tree more spectacular than the year before. I always feel under pressure to make it bigger and better and more wonderful, but this year something changed. I looked into the faces of my grandchildren and thought, this isn't what it's meant to be about. Christmas isn't a time for showing off. It's not a time to dwell on the material, although we do love presents, don't we?' Another ripple of laughter spread through the crowd. 'No, it's a time of sharing. So, with that in mind, I asked Tom and Jack here whether they'd like to decorate the tree with me. Of course, they were delighted and very generous too, because they've made all sorts of lovely things which they've hung on the branches. This year's tree, ladies and gentlemen, is a *family* tree.'

With that Hedda flicked the switch and Flappy stood aside to allow as many people as possible into the hall to see the tree. In they came, their faces alight with anticipation, and Flappy's heart went weak at the thought of them finding a mess of tinsel and crude cut-outs of Santa Claus and his reindeer and being disappointed. Yet, to her surprise, the comments that reached her ears were positive: 'charming', 'adorable', 'sweet'.

'How good of you, Flappy, to allow the children to decorate the tree,' said one, as she emerged from the house.

'What a lovely, lovely idea,' said another.

'The best tree you've ever done,' said a third.

And Flappy smiled the gracious smile for which she was so well known, and said, 'I am just so *so* lucky to have such delightful grandchildren. When it comes to decorating a Christmas tree, they are so much better at it than me.'

Then it was Charles, kissing her cheek and whispering

into her ear that he'd rather look at *her* than the tree, and if they were alone, he'd unwrap her like a present, and Flappy blushed the colour of Santa Claus's hat. It was a great relief to Flappy that she was *not* alone with Charles, for she would have liked nothing more than for Charles to unwrap her layer by layer until there was nothing left but her yielding body and irrepressible desire. 'Will you let me remove your wrapping, piece by piece?' he asked softly.

'Mum.' It was Jasper, tapping her on the shoulder from behind. 'Briony wants to let the children eat the chocolates on the tree. What do you say?'

Flappy looked deeply into Charles's eyes. She felt dizzy with joy, giddy with recklessness. 'Yes,' she said. 'Why not?'

And Flappy knew she had put one foot onto a very slippery slope.

Chapter 13

Once the Christmas drinks evening was over, Flappy could concentrate on Christmas Day. Really, the festive season was so exhausting! She had bought all the presents and Persephone had wrapped them up beautifully, following her instructions to the letter: green paper, red tartan ribbon and a sprig of fir tied into the knot. The effect was charming. Flappy had given Kenneth a list of suggestions for *her* Christmas presents. It wasn't very long because she couldn't think of anything she wanted that she didn't already have. Some cashmere, an Anya Hindmarch handbag, a Tiffany bracelet. Somehow, those things didn't excite her. She had shelves of cashmere, rows of designer bags and endless pretty bracelets. However, Kenneth took the list off with him when he climbed into his Jaguar and, as he wasn't dressed for golf, she assumed he was going shopping.

Flappy had taken trouble to decorate the house. Being a very popular person, possibly the *most* popular person in Badley Compton, she had received many cards. These she hung on a string in the hall, like bunting. She had a strong opinion about Christmas cards. The old-fashioned, traditional ones of nativity scenes and angels were proper and fitting. The modern ones, which displayed family photographs at their most glossy, were abhorrent. The word Flappy used, of course, was 'common'. In her opinion, the only family for whom it was appropriate to send such cards was the Royal Family. They'd been doing it for years. Indeed, it was because of them that the lesser folk had decided to do it, and what a disastrous decision that had been! The result was cheesy smiles, contrived poses and an undeniable air of smugness. If Flappy abhorred one thing, it was smugness! For these offenders Flappy had a separate string, hung up on a separate wall, which she called the string of shame.

The centrepiece of the hall was a large limestone and marble fireplace. Really, it was quite spectacular, the fireplace at Darnley, giving as it did a welcoming glow to those guests lucky enough to be invited for dinner. Flappy had adorned it with a thick garland of fir to which Persephone had attached gold pine cones and red velvet ribbons. The effect was, indeed, very pretty and Flappy lingered a moment to admire it. Her eyes lifted then to the portraits of Kenneth and herself that dominated the wall on either side of the fireplace. She was pleased to see that she hadn't aged much in the years since they had been painted. Thanks to hair dye and a healthy lifestyle she could still pass as a younger woman. Kenneth, on the other hand, had aged. But she didn't mind about that. Men improved with age and, although Kenneth wasn't handsome, he had a lively expression which made him attractive.

As much as she fancied Charles, and she really did fancy him *a lot*, Flappy knew she wouldn't swap her Toad for him were she given the chance. She and Toad were very happy.

How long, though, until she could persuade him to move back into his dressing room?

When Flappy and Kenneth weren't in the Caribbean spending Christmas with the entire family, they adhered to a programme at Darnley which had been conceived when the children were small. On Christmas Eve Kenneth became Father Christmas and placed the stockings, which Flappy (his Master Elf) had filled with presents, on the end of each child's bed. Since their children had flown the nest, Kenneth had not bothered to dress up as Father Christmas, but Flappy had continued the tradition and made him a stocking all the same. In return for his stocking, opened on Christmas morning at the breakfast table – for Flappy hated breakfast in bed on account of the mess – Kenneth gave Flappy a gift. (The year before last he had given her diamond earrings, which had been the fourth item on the list she had given him. The first being a new car, the second a set of crockery from Good Earth in Jaipur and the third a statue of a deer and its fawn for the garden.) After breakfast, they went to church for the Christmas service, sitting in their usual seats at the front with a clear view of the Christmas tree, which always came a poor second to Flappy's. After the service they returned home for lunch. In the years when it was just the two of them, they invited the Willises, and friends who, like them, were having a year off from their children and grandchildren. After lunch was the opening of gifts, which was the highlight of the day, although Flappy would never admit this. She maintained, always, that the church service with those uplifting carols and the Christmas message, delivered so eloquently by the vicar and the lesson readers, was what it was all about. She wasn't a materialistic woman, she insisted, but what sort of woman would she be if she failed to enter into the spirit of the consumer side of the festival? So enter in she did, with gusto.

This year, of course, she had Jasper and his family, which meant it was going to be much more fun. As much as she enjoyed Graham and Joan's company (well, to be honest, she didn't enjoy Joan's, she *tolerated* it) and the company of her friends, there was nothing like family. Hence, the table was laid for six and little baskets of sweets were put in front of Tom and Jack's places. Flappy sprinkled the table with silver and gold stars, planted the scented candles in nests of tinsel and hung the two stockings she had filled (with a teeny bit of help from Persephone) from the mantelpiece in the drawing room. After all, she *was* the Master Elf.

On Christmas morning, Flappy awoke at five o'clock feeling excited. She dressed for yoga in the bathroom so as not to awaken Kenneth, and tried hard not to resent him for making her creep out of the room in the dark. Christmas was no day to spend in resentment. After an hour of yoga and a sauna, she cooled off in the swimming pool, putting her hair up in a clip for she had had it blow-dried the day before and did not want to spoil it.

Wrapped in a towelling dressing gown she went into the kitchen and made herself a cup of tea with lemon, then wandered through the house turning on lights and admiring the rooms, for everything looked so festive and pretty. Outside, the sun was beginning to rise, shining weakly through the latticework of leafless trees and twinkling its Christmas greeting. A light frost lay on the grass, blue in the places where the sun couldn't reach, white and glittering in the places where it shone. The sky was pale and watery, a few strips of dove-grey cloud lingering beneath it like the remaining pieces of a storm. A flock of birds, disturbed by something on the ground, left the branches of a horse chestnut tree and took to the skies, inky black against the blue. Flappy stood at the drawing-room window, gazing out, and thought how beautiful nature was in the morning stillness, before humans stepped out to ruin it. And nowhere was more beautiful than Darnley.

Kenneth appeared at nine in a navy-blue dressing gown, his thin grey hair sticking up in wispy tufts. He looked like a schoolboy, shuffling in in slippers with a small box in his hand. 'Good morning, darling,' he said cheerfully, planting a kiss on Flappy's cheek. 'You smell nice.'

'Thank you, darling. Happy Christmas.' Flappy eyed the box and wondered whether it was the Tiffany bracelet she had put on her list. Kenneth sat down and Flappy made him his breakfast, as she did every morning. As there was no newspaper to read, they talked.

'Isn't it nice that we'll have Jasper this year,' he said.

'It's going to be lovely,' Flappy agreed. 'Christmas is really a festival for children, isn't it?'

'I agree.'

'I look forward to watching them opening their gifts.'

'Me too. That's the fun part.'

'The icing on the cake. A lot of work has gone into making the cake this year,' she said, enjoying the metaphor. 'Really, I've been run off my feet. It's nice to have finally got here, and everything is as it should be.'

Kenneth tucked into his egg and bacon on toast, while Flappy enjoyed yogurt with berries. He drank his coffee and Flappy sipped a cup of tea. Finally, when they'd finished eating, Kenneth pushed the little box across the table. He smiled at her, somewhat bashfully. 'This isn't on your list,' he said.

Flappy's heart took a dive. Kenneth never got it right if left to his own devices. Flappy had learned very early on in their marriage that, when it came to giving her presents, Kenneth should never *ever* be left to his own devices. Now, unfortunately, that rule had been broken. Not a good start to Christmas, she thought.

'How sweet of you, darling,' she said, smiling through her disappointment. 'I wonder what it could possibly be. You are naughty to go off on your own.'

'I know,' he said. 'But I had a little help.' Again, the bashful smile.

'Really?' she said, brightening. 'Did Persephone help you?'

'No, Briony did.'

'Oh,' she said again. This was confusing. Had Persephone helped she would have been certain to get a tasteful present, but Briony wasn't such a safe bet. Nonetheless, she slowly unwrapped it.

Inside was a little black box with pink ribbon. Theo

Fennell. She recognized the logo at once. Kenneth had likely never heard of Theo Fennell, the jeweller. Things were definitely looking up. Flappy pulled off the ribbon and opened the box. Inside, on a gold chain, was a key, encrusted with her favourite stones, diamonds, sapphires and emeralds. 'This is beautiful,' she gasped, surprised. Because it really was very beautiful. 'You're a darling, Toad. Thank you.'

'Your real present is yet to come,' he said, his smile widening. No longer bashful but excited.

'Really?' She narrowed her eyes. 'Kenneth?'

'It's not on your list,' he said, and by the look on his face she could tell that he was very proud of that fact.

'What have you done?'

'I said I would buy you something big and I have. Last year, when we flew out to the Caribbean, I could only take small things in my luggage. This year, we're here, so I can give you something that can't be squeezed into a suitcase.'

'How intriguing,' she said, wondering what on earth it could possibly be. 'In the meantime, here is your stocking. The Master Elf has been busy at work this Christmas.'

Kenneth opened each present with care, for the wrapping was a gift in itself. No one knew better than Flappy how to make a gift look sumptuous. He was just unwrapping the final gift, a pair of cufflinks made up of a golf ball and club, when there came the sound of singing from outside. Flappy looked at Kenneth and frowned. Kenneth looked at Flappy and frowned too. Neither particularly wanted to be caught in their dressing gowns. Flappy certainly did not want to be seen with her hair not done.

They got up together and went into the hall. Looking through the window they saw, to their surprise, Jasper, Briony and the boys standing in a row on the gravel with Buster, singing 'Silent Night'. They wore coats, hats and gloves, because it was bitingly cold in spite of the sunshine, and their breath misted on the air. Flappy still did not want to be seen in her dressing gown, but what could she do?

'They've come early,' said Kenneth.

'Yes, did you tell them to come at ten?'

'No.'

'Well ...' Flappy was going to tell Kenneth to send them home and then flee upstairs, but Kenneth was already opening the door and clapping. She could hardly run away now. Reluctantly forcing a smile onto her face, a smile that communicated her absolute joy and delight at seeing her family singing so beautifully in the forecourt, she joined Kenneth on the step and clapped. The children's faces flushed with pleasure. Jasper grinned proudly and Briony looked rather amazed to see her mother-in-law in such a state. It was rare to see her so unprepared, but there was something wonderfully nonchalant about it. It demonstrated to her how little Flappy really cared. How confident she was not to mind being seen *sans* make-up and with her hair fluffy, and how, in that state of naturalness, she looked so much younger. Had Flappy known these things she would have remained there for longer, but she didn't. As soon as they had finished and she had praised them heartily, she retreated upstairs to effect a transformation. Kenneth invited them in and they sat around the kitchen table and drank mugs of hot chocolate. Jasper gave Buster a bowl of milk.

At eleven o'clock they went to church. Flappy, with her hair perfectly coiffed beneath a scarlet hat which matched the scarlet coat she wore over a cashmere sweater and long skirt, led the way down the aisle. The usual seating arrangements did not apply at Christmas because various families were spending the festival elsewhere and others had invited their families to join them in Badley Compton, so that Jasper, Briony and the boys were able to take the pew behind Flappy and Kenneth.

Before sitting down, Flappy greeted Charles and Hedda, who were sitting with George and his siblings in the two front rows on the other side. Hedda, cheerful in a plum-coloured hat and navy-blue coat, wished her a happy Christmas and whispered in her ear that George was going to make an announcement at lunch. 'He's either getting married,' she hissed, 'or he's moving down here to stay. Either way, I'm beyond excited.'

'How marvellous,' Flappy hissed back, but she felt a pang of envy just beneath the ribs. How she wished that Jasper were going to make an announcement over lunch and declare that he'd found a wonderful job. Something glamorous. Something that Flappy could crow about, although it must be emphasized that Flappy was not a boastful woman. In fact, she abhorred boasting of any kind. But she was aware that, in life, there arose the odd occasion where boasting was not only unavoidable but absolutely necessary. The moment Jasper landed a job — not just *any* job, but a *good* job — would be one of those occasions. How she longed for it.

As she sat in her pew and took off her gloves, she sent a word up to the Good Lord. She knew she wasn't really in a position to ask for favours, considering her recent transgressions, but what harm could it do? *Ask and you will receive, that your joy may be complete.* John 16:24. She was doing nothing more than what was instructed in the Bible. She closed her eyes and asked. Then, as the vicar stepped into the middle of the nave, she hoped it wouldn't be long before her prayers were answered.

During the service, Charles tried to catch her eye, but Flappy's eye would not be caught. It would not be correct to flirt in church, on Christ's birthday. In fact, flirting in church was a definite no-no, and Flappy made every effort not to look at him. But Charles's gaze was hot and heavy and made her self-conscious. Of course, she was used to being looked at. Most of the locals looked at her, to see what she was wearing, to attract a smile or a nod of recognition, or simply to watch her as one might watch a famous person or someone one admires. This was a different kind of looking. Charles's looking demanded she look back, and it took a great deal of effort to keep her eyes trained in front of her, on Graham in his red robes, on the Christmas tree with its plastic angel planted crookedly on top, and on the choir of men and women from Badley Compton who sang with trembling voices, mostly out of tune, but definitely con brio.

Flappy wondered, as she knelt on the prayer cushion and clasped her hands together, whether Jasper was thinking of Molly and whether Molly was thinking of him. Was

Molly staring at the back of Jasper's head from the rear of the church as Charles was staring at Flappy? Were they in love or was it simply lust? Might Jasper's marriage be threatened? How terrible it would be for those two innocent boys if their parents separated on account of their father's inability to control his urges, Flappy thought, and then, when she realized she had missed the start of the prayers, pushed her worries to the back of her mind and tried to concentrate on what the vicar was saying. She had just asked a favour of God. Why would He oblige if she couldn't even be bothered to listen to the prayers. Contrite, she recited the Lord's Prayer in a loud voice so that the Good Lord would be in no doubt that she was not straying like a lost sheep.

After the service the congregants met outside the church as they always did. Today, however, there was a table of eggnog and roasted chestnuts and everyone mingled, though not for long, for they were eager to get home to their turkeys and Christmas puddings. Flappy had put the turkey in the oven at seven that morning and Karen had arrived just as they were leaving for church to prepare the rest of the lunch. Flappy moved around the crowd with efficiency, as an experienced queen does, wishing her friends a Merry Christmas, shaking hands with people she didn't know and graciously saying all the right things. By the look on the faces of those in receipt of her benevolence she was pleased she was able to spread some Christmas cheer.

Lunch was as entertaining as Flappy knew it would be. Jasper was full of jokes and colourful anecdotes. Briony laughed heartily at everything he said and praised Flappy's decorations so highly that Flappy forgot to be irritated by her Australian accent and the odd involuntary use of the word 'kids'. The boys gobbled up the turkey and all the trimmings and then did the same with the Christmas pudding, picking out the fifty-pence coins which, following tradition, Flappy had hidden inside. They stuffed their mouths with sweets and wriggled on their chairs, impatient for lunch to be over so they could open their presents.

Flappy thought of Hedda and Charles's Christmas lunch and wondered what George's announcement might be. She believed she would probably have heard from Persephone if he had asked her to marry him. Even though she hoped George was moving down to Badley Compton, she did not want to hear that he had acquired some wonderful job. She didn't think she could bear it. She abhorred jealousy more than anything else and yet, sometimes, in extreme situations, it was hard not to succumb to the green-eyed monster that lurks within us all. This was certainly an extreme situation, yet Flappy, who considered herself a good-natured person, was not proud of her jealousy.

When lunch was finally over, the family moved into the drawing room to open their presents. First, they started with the stockings hanging on the mantelpiece above the fireplace. The two boys tore at the paper, delighting in their gifts and squealing with excitement. Jasper and Briony looked on with pleasure, their faces alight with affection and appreciation for Grandma's generosity.

After the stockings had been discarded in a sea of

wrapping paper and ribbon, the children's attention turned to the presents at the foot of the tree in the hall. In and out of the drawing room they went, returning each time with a beautifully wrapped gift. Some were for Jasper and Briony, others were for Kenneth, most were for them. It wasn't until all the presents had been opened that Kenneth and Jasper left the room, returning a few minutes later with a large package, wrapped in brown paper. It looked like a painting or a mirror. Flappy was intrigued. Kenneth had said, after all, that he was going to buy her something big. Something special.

'This is for you, darling,' he said, beaming.

'But you've given me this beautiful key,' she said, running her fingers over it for it was now hanging around her neck and sparkling prettily against her skin. 'As well as all the things I put on my list. What more could I possibly want?'

Jasper grinned. 'You're going to want this!' he said.

'You know what it is?' Flappy asked.

'Of course. Dad and I plotted this together.'

'Actually,' said Briony. 'It was *my* idea.'

'That's true,' Jasper agreed. 'It was Briony's idea, but then Dad bought it.'

'Of course, he did,' said Flappy with a sigh. Jasper didn't have the wherewithal to earn the money to buy anything.

Kenneth and Jasper held it up as Flappy carefully unwrapped it, lifting the Sellotape off with care so as not to damage what was underneath. At last the back of a painting was revealed. The picture side faced the men. Flappy wondered what it could possibly be. She wasn't sure Kenneth could be trusted to buy a painting. She knew she'd have to fake being happy. If Flappy was good at one thing, it was faking being happy. She mentally prepared to give the performance of a lifetime.

The two men were grinning so much, Flappy's suspicions were aroused. Was this a joke? Was it some awful cartoon or a modern painting of an egg suspended in space? Slowly they turned it round. Her jaw dropped. She stared at the picture in amazement. It wasn't a picture but a portrait, of Jasper with his dog on his lap, and it was incredibly good. In fact, it was so good that Flappy knew at once that she'd hang it in the hall opposite the portraits of her and Kenneth.

'It's incredible!' she exclaimed, standing back to admire it from a distance. 'The artist has captured your personality so beautifully. Your humour, your wit, your sensitivity. Really, it's stunning. Who did it?' She peered into the bottom right-hand corner, then stared at Jasper in disbelief. 'Molly Price did this?'

'She did,' said Briony happily. 'We went to their house and she showed me her studio. She'd painted her children and Jim, so I thought it would be a great idea if she painted Jasper. Originally, I wanted it for me, but then Kenneth said he wanted it for you and, well, it just seemed right that you should have it, considering you already have two portraits in the hall.'

'She's very talented,' said Flappy, her voice heavy with admiration. She had clearly underestimated Molly Price.

'Yes, she is,' agreed Briony.

'Did you go to her studio to sit for her?' Flappy asked,

beginning to feel somewhat foolish. When Molly was touching Jasper's face at the jumble sale, it must have been to do with the portrait.

'Yes, quite a few times, actually,' said Jasper. 'Then Dad bought the frame.'

'I knew you'd want to hang it in the hall, so it had to match ours,' said Kenneth.

'It certainly does that,' said Flappy excitedly. She looked at her husband with affection. 'You are a darling Toad,' she said, her eyes filling with tears. 'It's the most wonderful present you could ever give me.'

'It's a pleasure.' Kenneth flushed with happiness as Flappy planted a kiss on his cheek.

'Perhaps she can paint the boys next,' said Briony. 'For Flappy's birthday. What do you say?' She smiled in that breezy way of hers and turned to Jasper for approval, but really, it was going to be Kenneth who would pay.

'I have an announcement to make,' said Jasper, looking once again at his mother.

An announcement? Flappy couldn't believe it. Had the Good Lord listened to her, after all? She held her breath.

'I am starting a business.' This was not music to his mother's ears but a whole symphony. 'George and I have bought The Happy Prawn and are going to open a new restaurant called Jasper and George.'

Flappy looked at Kenneth, for Jasper didn't have the money to buy a restaurant. 'Charles and I have invested in it,' Kenneth told her. So, that's what they were doing in town, *not* buying a house for Briony. Flappy was relieved.

'Darling, that is wonderful news,' she cried, throwing her arms around her son.

'We'll need you, Mum, to help with the decor. No one has good taste like you do. Will you help?'

'Of course, I will,' she replied. If anyone knew how best to decorate a restaurant, it was Flappy.

Flappy sank into the sofa and wondered how she was going to let her friends know about Jasper's exciting new job without appearing boastful. Boastfulness was born out of a sense of lack and right now Flappy lacked nothing. In fact, her world was complete. More complete than it had ever been. As her busy mind stilled to give her space in which to enjoy the moment, a cunning idea popped into the void. *I'll arrange a coffee morning with the ladies at Big Mary's*, she thought with satisfaction. *That way everyone in Badley Compton will have heard all about it by lunchtime.* And with this simple strategy in place, Flappy knew that she would propagate the good news with as much success as she had withheld the bad. She gazed lovingly across the room at Jasper and wondered how she could ever have doubted him.

Chapter 14

As soon as Christmas was over Flappy and Hedda met in Flappy's little sitting room, a harmonious and peaceful room decorated in green floral designs with windows looking out onto the box garden. The fire flickered hospitably in the grate and the two friends sat before it in comfortable armchairs, drinking cups of tea. Flappy had put a plate of biscuits on the table, through which Hedda was slowly working her way. Flappy, who was focused on shedding a final half-pound, refrained.

'It came as such as surprise,' said Flappy.

'Me too,' Hedda agreed. 'I thought he was going to announce his engagement.'

'Perhaps it's a teeny bit early for an engagement.'

'Of course, it is. But I couldn't imagine what else it could be.'

'All those games of golf and tennis and I thought Jasper was just having fun.'

'You know many a business deal is made that way,' Hedda pointed out. 'Golf is an ideal sport for networking.'

'And there was I, lamenting the fact that my son had no drive or ambition.'

'You clearly underestimated him,' said Hedda with a smile.

'I did.' Flappy poured more tea. 'Jasper and George is a wonderful idea and I'm sure it will be very popular. Both those young men have everything it takes to make a success of it.' She looked at Hedda, her dear friend Hedda, and felt the need to unburden her conscience. 'I have to make a confession, Hedda. You are the only person I can talk to honestly.'

Hedda raised her eyebrows. 'All right,' she said and narrowed her eyes. Flappy wondered suddenly whether she thought she was going to confess something about Charles and realized she'd better be hasty and put her mind at rest. Thank goodness, this time it had nothing to do with him.

'I thought Jasper was having an affair with Molly Price.'

Hedda burst out laughing. 'Jasper having an affair? Oh, Flappy! Jasper is clearly devoted to Briony. Everyone can see that. And he simply doesn't have it in him to be disloyal. He's a morally upright sort of person. A paragon of integrity.'

'I know. It was silly of me. But when Andy, our head gardener, went to help her with her garden, he reported that he'd seen Jasper there. When I mentioned it, Briony seemed to have no idea that he'd even been to her house and, when I investigated further, I discovered that he was going there all the time. Jim wasn't home, so I put two and two together . . .'

'And made ten,' Hedda interrupted.

'I feel very foolish now.'

203

'Did you ever ask him what he was doing at Molly's house?'

'Yes, I did mention it once, in a subtle way.'

'What did he say?'

'That he was helping her with her interior design.' Flappy pulled a face. It did seem ridiculous now, with hindsight.

Hedda laughed again. 'That's hilarious!' she exclaimed. 'I can't imagine Jasper knows anything about interior design.'

'He doesn't,' Flappy agreed, enjoying the funny side of it now that the danger had passed. 'His taste is almost as bad as Kenneth's.' The two women laughed heartily.

'I imagine you worked yourself up into quite a lather,' said Hedda, wiping a tear from beneath one eye.

'I did. I couldn't tell Kenneth. I couldn't tell anyone. I was so ashamed that my son could betray his family.'

'I do think it's irresponsible and selfish to give into one's desires in that way when one has a wife and children who will be hurt if one gets caught,' said Hedda thoughtfully. 'But when the children have flown the nest and have husbands and wives of their own, I don't see anything wrong with it, as long as one is discreet.' She looked at Flappy and smiled. 'We live a long time these days, long enough to have many lives, really. I don't think it's fair to expect one's spouse to stay faithful for ever.'

Flappy could not disagree, not in front of Hedda, who knew all about her affair with Charles. 'The key is discretion,' she said carefully, not wanting to bring up that painful moment of being caught kissing in the garden.

'It is, indeed, Flappy. What the eye doesn't see, the heart doesn't grieve for, isn't that so?'

'I don't think Kenneth has it in him to have an affair.'

'Not like Charles. Goodness, he's always in love with somebody.'

Flappy was certain that Hedda was wrong. Charles was in love with *her* and had given no indication that he would stop being in love with her. Perhaps, once, he had moved from woman to woman like a bee in a flower border, but his heart was in *her* hands now – it was only a shame that his body couldn't be. 'Would *you* ever stray from the marital bed?' Flappy asked boldly.

Hedda bit into the biscuit and chewed for a moment, as if weighing up the pros and cons of confessing such intimate secrets to Flappy. 'I *have* done on two occasions and would do so again if the right man came along. The trouble is, what starts as a jolly flirt and a roll in the hay ends up in demands. The trick is to find someone who doesn't make demands, who just wants the fun. I really have no desire to entangle myself in something that then becomes a bore because he wants too much of me. I'll never leave Charles, ever. I just don't want to sleep with him.'

How very aristocratic, thought Flappy, impressed. Only an aristocrat would speak candidly with such nonchalance about extramarital affairs. It was in their culture, after all, wasn't it?

'It's just boring having sex with someone one's been married to for forty years,' Hedda continued, warming to her subject. 'The fun of sex is in the discovering of each other, not in the familiar. I'm afraid children and domesticity kill one's desire. You know the saying: "Show me a beautiful woman and I'll show you a man who's tired of sleeping with her." It works the other way round. My husband is possibly the most handsome man on the planet and yet I'm bored to death of sleeping with him.'

Flappy couldn't imagine ever getting bored of sleeping with Charles. 'But you love him,' she said. 'I understand that. Love and sex are two very different things and not dependent on each other.'

'Indeed not.' Hedda grinned and Flappy saw mischief in it. 'Between you and me, I'd love to find some devilishly attractive man in Badley Compton to entertain me a couple of times a week. But while I'm looking, I enjoy Charity Chance's erotic novels. They take the edge off what is sometimes an uncomfortable longing.'

'Oh, Hedda!' Flappy laughed, half thrilled, half appalled by her friend's admission of sexual craving.

'We might be getting older, Flappy, but that doesn't mean we don't still want the attentions of a man.'

'It is true, although, *I* had my fingers burnt. I don't think I'll be doing that again.' Flappy, *not* being aristocratic, was less comfortable speaking about infidelity and was now keen to change the subject.

Hedda smiled knowingly. 'Never say never, dear friend. You're a beautiful woman and you're married to a man who spends his life on the golf course. You're entitled to a bit of fun, you know. You deserve to be admired and adored. We *all* do. But when one is young like Jasper, with small children and an adoring wife, it's not on, is it?'

Flappy was relieved the conversation was moving back to

Jasper's mistaken adultery. 'I was so happy when I discovered that Jasper hadn't been having an affair, only having his portrait painted,' she said.

'It's a very good portrait,' said Hedda, helping herself to another biscuit. 'Molly's talented.'

'Very talented. It looks good up there in the hall, doesn't it?'

'You'll have to have your other children painted.'

'That won't happen. They never come home these days.' Flappy sighed regretfully as she thought of Daniel and the girls. 'Sadly, I see precious little of them, living as they do at different ends of the world. At least they remembered to call us on Christmas Day. No, I don't think I'll be commissioning portraits of *them*.'

'Jack and Tom then. There's plenty of room beside Jasper.'

'That would be nice, although I'll have to fight their mother to have it hung here at Darnley.'

'And I imagine she can put up quite a fight. She's a tough girl, that one.'

Flappy inhaled through her nose. Indeed, she was.

As soon as it was possible Flappy met the ladies at Big Mary's. Mabel had suggested they meet at Flappy's because they wanted to see the new portrait of Jasper, but Flappy insisted on going to Café Délice because everyone who was anyone went there and she couldn't wait to tell them about Jasper and George's new venture. Flappy assured them that they'd get to see the portrait at her *ballo in maschera*. Everyone else would be directed to the tent via the garden, but the ladies, being her best friends, would be permitted to go via the house. They were a little disappointed, but knew better than to argue with Flappy. Flappy was not a woman to be argued with.

As usual, the five women were given the round table in the window. In spite of the cold, and it was exceedingly cold that Christmas, the sunshine streamed in through the glass and warmed them up a little. They hugged their mugs of coffee and devoured the cakes, while Flappy, mindful of that final, stubborn half-pound and the wedding dress that waited to reveal whether or not her efforts had been successful, held back. 'I have some wonderful news,' she said, simply bursting with excitement to share it.

'I love wonderful news!' gushed Mabel.

'Is it about Jasper?' asked Sally. 'We've been waiting to hear.'

'It is and I'm so *so* proud.' Flappy gave a little sniff, held steady their gazes and then delivered it in exactly the way she had fantasized about delivering it for weeks. 'Jasper and George Harvey-Smith are going into business together. They've bought The Happy Prawn and are renaming it Jasper and George. It's going to be the most wonderful new restaurant. Those two together are dynamite.'

The ladies were visibly impressed. 'Well, that *is* a surprise,' gushed Esther. 'I could never have predicted it.'

'The Happy Prawn is a great location,' said Madge. 'I go there a lot. I like the view of the sea and the prawns are always happy,' she said with a giggle.

'Jasper recommended I steer clear of the prawns when we dined there last month,' Flappy told her. 'Jasper and George's prawns will be a great deal happier, I can assure you.'

'How exciting!' enthused Sally. 'I mean, it's really good news. They must have been plotting for some time. These things don't happen overnight.'

'Lots of wheeling and dealing on the golf course,' said Flappy, remembering what Hedda had told her. 'You know that's where most business deals are made. Either on the golf course or the tennis court.' She was *not* going to tell them that Charles and Kenneth were the two investors. She wanted them to think that the boys had done it on their own. 'They've asked me to advise on the decor. I'm incredibly busy, but I'm sure I can give them some tips.'

'Oooh! It's going to be sumptuous!' Mabel cried.

'It'll be good for Badley Compton to have a sophisti-cated restaurant,' said Madge, who knew that if Flappy was even a little bit involved, it would be the height of refinement.

'What kind of food will they serve?' asked Esther.

'The very best,' said Flappy, who didn't know. 'Fresh fish. Healthy Mediterranean food. Jasper loves his food. You can be sure it'll be to everyone's taste.'

'When will it open?' asked Mabel. 'I can hardly wait!'

Flappy didn't know that either. 'In the spring,' she guessed, because spring was a time of renewal.

'Do you think we'll have our coffee mornings there?' Sally asked.

Flappy hadn't thought of that. 'We must tread carefully,'

she warned, glancing at Big Mary. 'We don't want to offend. I must tell Jasper that he's not to take customers away from here.'

'It's a delicate balance,' said Esther. 'And you, Flappy, are going to be walking a tightrope.'

Flappy was well aware of her power. 'I will promote Jasper and George while at the same time give my support to Big Mary.' She smiled, the smile of a queen who knows her duty. 'I'm sure the two establishments can co-exist very comfortably together. This town is big enough for both.'

However, she couldn't help but think that Big Mary might be a little put out at the news. Even though one was a café and the other a restaurant, there was no doubt in Flappy's mind that Jasper and George would become the most popular venue in town. After having wanted to spread the news as quickly as possible, Flappy was now keen to leave without having spread it further than her table. She did not want to be the one to tell Big Mary.

Flappy made a point of telephoning Molly to thank her for painting Jasper so beautifully. 'I had no idea how talented you are,' she told her. 'But now I know, I'm going to recommend you to all my friends.' Molly thanked her. As well she might, Flappy thought grandly, because one word from *her* and the great and good of Badley Compton would rush to follow her lead and commission Molly to paint portraits for *them*. 'Before you get booked up,' Flappy added, bearing this in mind, 'I'd love you to paint my grandchildren.'

Molly replied with enthusiasm. 'Thank you, Flappy. I'd be honoured.' And Flappy hung up, pleased with herself for helping Molly find work. After all, it was nothing for Flappy but it would mean so much to Molly.

Persephone came to work in the days between Christmas and New Year because there were many last-minute things she had to do with regard to Flappy's *ballo in maschera*. While Flappy kept a sharp eye on all the arrangements, it was Persephone who toiled. In the three days preceding the ball Darnley Manor became a hive of activity once again. Trucks came and went delivering tables and chairs, crockery and cutlery. The Italian-inspired marquee was put up on the croquet lawn. Portaloos were positioned behind it. The florist arrived with extravagant displays, Venetian glass vases and miniature Lion of Venice statues to be placed in the centre of each table. The theatre company Persephone had so cleverly found began to create Venice inside the tent. There were enormous screens depicting the city, arched wooden bridges complete with iron lamps attached to the balustrades, layers of bubble wrap gave the illusion of water in the canals and a couple of gold-painted gondolas with crimson velvet cushions floated serenely upon it. The ceiling of the tent was black and studded with tiny lights, resembling stars.

Flappy was thrilled with the effect and she couldn't wait for the day to arrive when she'd stand with Kenneth at the grand entrance in her magnificent dress and mask and greet all her friends and acquaintances, and the one or two 'borderlines' she'd allowed to slip through the net. How impressed everyone was going to be.

The day before the ball, Flappy decided to try on her wedding dress. It had only been six weeks since she had started working out and dieting with the intention of losing the weight, but she hoped, with her fast metabolism and determination, that those pounds would have fallen off. She wanted to look and feel her best at the ball. Extra flesh around her hips and thighs would, without doubt, rob her of her confidence and panache.

Her chest tight with apprehension she made her way to the room at the end of the corridor and closed the door behind her. She didn't want Kenneth to find her trying on her wedding dress. He wouldn't understand. He might even assume that she wanted to renew her wedding vows. Flappy loved Kenneth, but she had no intention of doing that. Renewing one's wedding vows at their age was very common.

Once again, she slipped out of her clothes and into the dress. She could feel it was looser as she pulled it over her thighs and bottom. When she attempted the zip, it closed without straining the fabric. Well, if she was honest – and, standing alone in front of panels of mirrors made it hard *not* to be honest – there was a teeny bit of straining. But only a bit. Nothing to worry about. Nothing to dampen her spirits. It could be, perhaps, a little water retention.

Flappy was satisfied. She went straight to the kitchen and celebrated with a piece of toast. Flappy never *ever* ate toast in the middle of the day. She rarely touched wheat at all. But in celebration of her success, she spread a thin layer of peanut butter on a piece of toasted granary bread and relished every delicious bite of it.

As Flappy contemplated the new year, she thought how lucky she had been this past year. In fact, when she started to count the wonderful things that had happened to her she had to stop; there were simply too many blessings to put onto a list. However, a few things stood out and she contemplated them with gratitude. Jasper had found a job and not just any job but a job with all the glamour and prestige Flappy had wished for. Persephone wouldn't be leaving for London. George had returned to Badley Compton where he would be staying. Flappy was sure he would eventually ask Persephone to marry him. But right now, all that mattered was that she wasn't going to leave. Flappy had dreaded it. She had not only grown dependent on the girl, but had become incredibly fond of her too. It would have broken her heart to see her go. Flappy didn't think she could be in arrears anymore with God, for if she were, He would surely not have bestowed upon her so much good fortune.

The night before the ball, Kenneth and Flappy dined together in the kitchen. Flappy had lit a candle and placed it on the table, giving the evening an unusually romantic feel. Karen had cooked a chicken curry and Flappy had heated it up and prepared steamed rice and vegetables to go with it. Food was important to Kenneth, while Flappy would have been happy with a boiled egg.

'This is good,' he said, forking another heap of curry into his mouth and chewing happily. 'You're a wonderful cook, Flappy.'

Flappy did not correct him. 'I'm glad you like it,' she said.

'It's been a good year, hasn't it,' he reflected, washing the curry down with a slurp of claret.

'It's been exceedingly good. In fact, I don't think I could have asked for a better one. Well, it would have been nice to have seen Daniel and the girls.'

'It would, but we'll all get together next year in St Barts.'

Flappy frowned. The only reason they came to St Barts was because Kenneth paid for them. 'I think they should come here,' she said firmly. 'They haven't been home for years. I think their children should see Darnley. It's the family home, after all. Having Jasper here for Christmas this year has shown me how important it is for us to be together, here, in the place where they grew up.'

'It would make a nice change,' said Kenneth thoughtfully, topping up his glass.

'I'm not saying we should stop going to St Barts altogether, only that every other year you put your hand in your pocket and give them the holiday of a lifetime. Enough now. It's about time they did something for you. For *us*.'

'You're quite right, darling. This year has proved how lovely Christmas at home can be. How much more complete it would be with the *whole* family.'

Flappy put her hand on his. 'Thank you, Toad,' she said.

'For what?'

214

'For supporting me.'

He smiled, searching her face for the reason why she had suddenly become emotional. 'But of course.'

'I love my portrait of Jasper, but more than that I love the thought behind it. The fact that you and Jasper, and Briony, of course, plotted behind my back to have it painted.'

'We wanted to give you something special.'

'Well, you achieved that, and more. I'm really touched, Kenneth.' Flappy's eyes shone and she smiled to hide just how touched she was, and relieved, because all her fears had evaporated.

'I'm glad, because you do so much for us, it's only right that we should do something for you for a change. You are one in a million, Flappy.'

Flappy's breath caught in her throat. 'Oh, Toad . . .'

Kenneth shovelled the last of the curry into his mouth and glanced at the oven to see if there might be more. Flappy stood up and went to serve him another helping, grateful to have a moment to compose herself. When she came back her eyes were dry and her smile steady.

'And Jasper's got a job, at last,' she said, sitting down.

'Yes, good idea, don't you think.'

'Whose was it?'

'Persephone's.'

Flappy frowned. 'Persephone came up with the idea of buying a restaurant?'

'They went for dinner there and Persephone heard from one of the waitresses that the owner was wanting to retire.'

'And she told the boys to buy it?'

'I suppose she must have done.'

'Isn't she wonderful!' Flappy exclaimed, ever more admiring of her. 'She said nothing about it to me.'

'Because she's discreet,' said Kenneth. 'She knows how to keep a secret.'

Flappy lowered her eyes. 'She certainly does,' she agreed, pushing *that* particular secret to the back of her mind.

Kenneth drained his glass, put his napkin on the table and leaned back in his chair. 'I've had quite a lot to drink tonight, darling,' he said, stifling a belch. 'I think I'll sleep in my dressing room.'

And there it was! Flappy's Christmas was complete.

Chapter 15

The night of the *ballo in maschera* could not have been more perfect. There were no clouds to mar the splendour of the skies, no rain to dampen the ground, not even a wind to whistle through the bare branches of the horse chestnut trees and unsettle the birds roosting among them. All was still and quiet and strangely magical, as if a supernatural power had cast a spell over the land and suspended winter's usual drama. The many gardens of Darnley Manor, of which Flappy was so deeply proud, were lit up with a thousand fairy lights twinkling enticingly through the crisp, frosty air, and above them a million stars glittered in an indigo sky. Badley Compton had never witnessed such a spectacle nor had such pleasure dressing up.

As Jack and Tom and the Price children ran amok through the marquee, dressed more like Victorian pickpockets than eighteenth-century urchins, Flappy stood at the entrance, in a gold and silver dress of such beauty that it would find no competition tonight, not even in the younger women whose dresses had also been made by Esmeralda Trott. Esmeralda had made sure of that. Tonight was Flappy's night to shine and shine she did, like the brightest star. As if the dress were not enough, the top half of her face was concealed by a fabulous mask, painted gold to match her dress and adorned with a thick spray of purple and gold feathers. She stood beside Kenneth whose costume, designed to match hers, was so over the top with its brocading and trimmings that he looked quite ridiculous. However, Kenneth was delighted. He loved fancy dress and the more outrageous it was, the happier *he* was. The whole point, surely, was to have fun. Flappy was used to her husband's penchant for flamboyant dressing and thought he looked every bit the portly Venetian gentleman and, anyway, tonight was not about Kenneth, it was about *her.*

Jasper and Briony carried their costumes well. Briony was top to toe in scarlet with a gold and feather mask, while Jasper had come as Harlequin, his face painted to look like a clown. Molly and Jim had also made an effort, but the results were less flamboyant than their friends'. Molly was in a pink and yellow dress, which made her look a touch matronly, while her husband was in black, his entire face covered by a rather sinister-looking mask. Flappy hoped they were keeping an eye on their children and making sure they weren't jumping in and out of the gondolas and popping the bubble wrap.

Flappy was most proud of Persephone, who, in the sumptuous blue and green dress Esmeralda had fashioned for her, looked like a Venetian princess of both class and beauty. Flappy watched her bustle about the tables, checking that everything was as it should be, and felt a tremendous surge of affection. How close she had come to losing her to London. What a blow that would have been. Flappy must have done something right for the Good Lord to have blessed her so.

At last the guests began to arrive, parking their cars in the field and walking towards the marquee along a path illuminated by elegant Venetian street lamps. Flappy's stomach fluttered with nerves as she saw them approach. In fact, she felt as if she had a whole flock of birds in there, trying to get out. Kenneth wasn't nervous at all, as unlike his wife he never thought about all the things that could go wrong. He simply turned up at the given time and enjoyed himself. However, as soon as the first arrivals reached the marquee, the birds in Flappy's stomach settled down and she embraced her guests warmly, soaking up the compliments that came thick and fast.

'*Benvenuti*,' Flappy exclaimed joyfully, and, because it wasn't gracious to take without giving, she added, 'What wonderful costumes! Everyone has made such an effort.' And it was true, they had. No one would have dared turn up to Flappy's *ballo in maschera* in anything less than a full costume, complete with wig, mask and buckled shoes.

Soon the marquee was heaving with guests. They swept their eyes over the giant backdrops that gave the impression that they were in St Mark's Square, walked over the arched bridges and admired the gondolas floating on the canal and the handsome *gondolieri* who stood inside them, oars in hand as if ready to push off and float away. Flappy had not missed a single detail and the effects left many of the guests almost speechless with admiration. 'No one could do this but you, Flappy,' they said when they found their voices, and Flappy accepted their praise with her usual humility, because she was, undoubtedly, a woman who had learned through hours of meditation to rise above the cravings of the ego. 'I did have a teeny bit of help from my personal assistant,' she told them grandly, and only because she liked Persephone did she give her credit for the hard work she had done.

Flappy felt a pair of hands grab her around the waist from behind. She knew instantly to whom they belonged. 'Charles,' she said, spinning round. Charles was wearing a dashing costume that made him look more like Zorro than a masked Venetian. His trousers were black and, Flappy noticed, beautifully cut. His shirt was white with a ruffle down the front, a black cloak was hooked onto his shoulders. His mask was menacing, being as dark as night and covering the top half of his face. Through two round holes his eyes gleamed a demonic green. Flappy's gaze fell to his mouth, his full, sensual mouth that she had kissed so many times, and she felt giddy with desire. Here she was, in her finery, high on compliments and excitement, and she wanted more than anything to fall into his arms and to give herself to him, impatiently, eagerly, hungrily. Yet, she couldn't. She had vowed that she wouldn't and she would stick to that vow, because Flappy was a woman who stood by vows when she knew what she might lose were she to break them.

'Just the sight of you arouses me, Beauty,' he breathed, pressing his cheek against hers and whispering into her ear.

He inhaled her perfume with a greedy sniff. Flappy could feel his lips brush her neck.

'Not here,' she replied, gently pushing him away and glancing around to see if they were being observed. After all, she was the hostess and it was natural that everyone wanted to look at her. She flicked open her fan and began to wave it in front of her face.

'I need to see you,' he said and his tone was urgent, as if the consequences of *not* seeing her would be intolerable.

Flappy took a sharp breath. She had drunk only one glass of champagne. However, it wasn't the alcohol that made her reckless, but the mask. It was as if she were not herself but someone else entirely – a beautiful Venetian woman with no ties, flirting with an admirer she'd only just met, in the romantic atmosphere of Piazza San Marco. 'Later,' she heard herself say. How easy it was, suddenly, to forget about her vow.

'One o'clock in the cottage,' came the reply. Those demonic eyes bored into her. They would accept no refusal tonight. Intoxicated with the magic of this magnificent ball, and her undeniable success, Flappy was in no position to refuse Beastie.

She felt herself tremble and give him a nod.

Charles's lips curled into a smile and he turned on his heel and disappeared into the throng. Flappy immediately regretted it. What was she thinking? She swallowed hard and went to find Kenneth. As long as she was with Kenneth, she would behave herself.

Kenneth was talking to Graham, who had come dressed as

221

the Pope. Perfect, thought Flappy. If anyone could save her from herself it was the Pope. 'Good evening, Your Holiness,' she said, bobbing a curtsey.

Graham was thrilled. 'Ah, the beautiful hostess,' he replied, bowing. 'You are the belle of the ball.'

'Surely not,' said Flappy, knowing very well that she was.

'What a party,' he exclaimed, shaking his head because he couldn't find words that did justice to the wonder of it. And if *he*, the vicar, had trouble articulating his appreciation, what hope was there for the rest of them?

'Flappy never disappoints,' said Kenneth, grinning at her over his golden goblet of champagne. 'Do we know those chaps in the gondolas? They look very familiar.'

'Persephone found them,' Flappy replied. 'I imagine they might be friends of hers.'

'I think they're from the golf club,' Kenneth added. 'I think one of them has carried my clubs.'

'It's good of you to give the local people work,' said Graham, dropping his Pope voice and speaking in his vicarish one instead.

Flappy, who had no idea who the *gondolieri* were, smiled benevolently. 'One does one's best to support the community.'

'And may I congratulate you on Jasper's new venture,' he said and Flappy beamed with pleasure.

'You may indeed,' she replied.

A moment later she was surrounded by Mabel, Esther, Madge and Sally, who were so keen to tell her what they thought of her party that they all talked at once and Flappy could barely make out what they were saying. However, she was in no doubt that she had pulled off a triumph. 'You really are the bravest woman I know,' said Sally, who had come as a courtesan. Although, to be fair, she didn't look much like a courtesan and one might not have known had she not gone around telling everyone.

Esther had come dressed as a man in a purple velvet jacket, matching knickerbockers and a giant white wig. 'Everyone will talk about tonight for years to come,' she said, and Flappy frowned, wondering why she had chosen not to wear a dress.

'Did you arrive on a horse?' she asked.

Esther laughed. 'Now that would have been fun. Why didn't I think of that?'

'Everyone's talking about Jasper and George's restaurant,' Mabel cut in, knowing that Flappy would be pleased to hear that. And indeed she was. Flappy's eyes shone with happiness. Not only was her party a great success, but she was basking too in Jasper's reflected glory just as she had longed to do. Her gaze drifted across the room and she caught Charles's dark stare through his mask. Flappy had indicated with a nod, a teeny but unmistakable nod, that she would meet him at the cottage at one. He was holding her to it, she could tell. That look was reminding her of her commitment, daring her to honour it. What was she to do? Half of her wanted to meet him – no, *more* than half, three-quarters, to be accurate – the other quarter did not. She averted her eyes and turned back to the ladies. However, the small voice of her conscience was drowned out by the louder voice of her desire, made reckless beneath the fantasy of her costume.

Flappy circulated as a good hostess is duty-bound to do,

charming everyone, even those borderline couples who had only succeeded in being invited on account of Flappy's generosity of spirit. Had her mood at the time of making the list been a degree less cheery they would have found themselves gazing longingly at the fireworks lighting up the sky above Darnley from their cold sitting rooms in Badley Compton. Flappy, in turn, was rewarded for her altruism by their unwavering loyalty, for such was their gratitude at being included in this exclusive event that they would remain forever her devoted servants.

At dinner, Flappy had placed herself between Graham and George. She was glad she hadn't put herself next to Charles. That would have been too much. It was enough that he was sitting in her line of vision at the table next to hers, trying to catch her eye every time she looked in his direction.

Kenneth hosted a table, seated beside Hedda and Mabel. Jasper hosted one too, but Flappy had not put him next to Molly, just in case an inappropriate frisson had sparked between them during all those sittings. She had placed Briony next to Charles and Jim, with Persephone on Jim's other side, because even though Jim had found his tongue, he was still hard to place, and who but Briony and Persephone could abide him?

Flappy might have come to her senses during her conversation with Graham. There was nothing like a vicar to remind her of her duty as a wife and mother and to deter her from straying, again, into Charles's embrace. But she noticed, as her eyes wandered to Charles, that he was no longer watching *her*, but flirting with Briony. Briony did, indeed, look ravishing, Flappy could not deny that. To Flappy's dismay, Charles was no longer trying to catch her attention, but quite obviously captivated by the young beauty in scarlet sitting on his right. He was laughing at everything Briony said, and she, in turn, was clearly relishing his conversation. Flappy knew just how witty and charming Charles could be. She felt her stomach clench with jealousy – jealousy which Flappy so abhorred, being so very beneath her, but she could not suppress the green eye of her competitive spirit. How could Charles, who only a moment ago had been gazing longingly in her direction, now gaze longingly at her daughter-in-law?

The tables looked spectacular with their extravagant floral centrepieces and Lion of Venice statues placed high on plinths. The ceiling sparkled with thousands of tiny lights and it really did feel as if they were in Venice, on a balmy summer's night. The caterers had done an excellent job and the food was original and delicious. After dinner Kenneth gave a speech and everyone raised their glasses to Flappy. Flappy, who was used to adulation, was surprisingly moved. Could it have been that, in that moment of appreciation, she felt the cold hand of fate squeeze her heart as the clock ticked on towards one o'clock? Like Cinderella, was this beautiful fantasy about to turn to rags? Even though, *un*like Cinderella, she had the power to stop it. Did she want to?

After dinner there was dancing. Kenneth swept Flappy onto the dance floor and all the while she was in his arms, she was thinking about Charles and Briony and hoping they weren't dancing together. She strained her neck to see, but there were so many masked guests jumping about – really, it was like a kaleidoscope of colour – that she was unable to make them out. Had they perhaps gone for a walk in the garden? The competitive spirit inside of Flappy, ignited during dinner, was now on fire. Gone were the good intentions, the adherence to vows, the promises to herself and to her God. Flappy was determined as only Flappy could be to make that one o'clock rendezvous and to remind Charles of all the reasons he loved her. As Kenneth manoeuvred her into a Carousel Twirl she thought about the terrible sins she was about to commit: the sin of breaking her vow; the sin of betraying her husband; the sin of breaking her promise to Hedda. And yet, she was unable to control the flames of both her desire and her sense of competition. At one o'clock she would give in to Charles and to her own uncontrollable longing. She couldn't hope that Persephone would save her a second time. No, this time she was well and truly lost.

At a quarter to one Flappy left the tent and sneaked off into the garden. The moon was a glowing marble ball illuminating her way, but even if it had been less bright she knew the terrain so well she would have found it all the same. She did not take the usual path, which was lit by hundreds of tea lights for those enamoured couples who might like to stroll beneath the stars. She went via the rose garden which, now it was winter, was asleep beneath the soil.

There was frost upon the ground. Her breath misted on the air. It was so quiet she could hear her footsteps crunching on the crusty grass and her heartbeat thumping in her chest. She wouldn't get caught, she told herself. Few knew about the cottage, fewer still knew where the key was hidden, and no one would think of visiting it tonight, not when Venice held more charm. She had been restrained all these months while Charles had tried to wear her down. She had been loyal to her husband and to Hedda, but now, on this night of illusion and theatre, she would cast aside her loyalty for one time and one time only. It would be a moment of passion and nothing more. She would return to the party and to her life and in the morning, when the masks had come off and sunlight exposed her *ballo in maschera* as being nothing but a beautiful dream, she would pretend it never happened. No one would be any the wiser. The Venetian queen who had made love to the masked stranger in black in the cottage at the bottom of the garden would not have really existed, but would have been an illusion, as false as a reflection on water. How wonderfully romantic that sounded, like a fairy tale.

Flappy's body was warm with the anticipation of Charles's touch. She hadn't wrapped herself in fur, but stepped into the crisp night in nothing but her dress and her mask. However, the cold could not compete with her blood that ran hot and fast through her veins. As she hurried through the garden her shallow breath grew shallower still as the neglected nerves in the dark and secret corners of her body stirred with the expectation of all the deliciously naughty ways in which they would soon be aroused. Charles was a skilful and generous lover and Flappy, now quickening her pace, was reminded, by the ache now spreading through her loins, just how skilful and generous he was and her impatience to hold him intensified.

When the cottage at last came into view she was surprised to see candlelight glowing in the window. How thoughtful of Charles to think of that, she mused. Her spirits soared with delicious anticipation and she quickened her pace. However, as she got nearer, her attention was distracted by a figure of a man in black hurrying down the path, as dark as a shadow, making his way eagerly towards the cottage door. Flappy stopped in her tracks. If Charles was *outside*, who had lit the candles *inside*? She frowned in confusion. She remained still and watched him open the door and step inside. As he did so, Flappy distinctly saw a flash of scarlet and the figure of a woman, then the door was closed and the two of them were gone from her sight.

Now she was enraged. How dare Charles betray her in this way? How dare he humiliate her! Why invite her to meet him at the cottage if he was meeting someone else there? But then her confusion mounted. Who was the woman who had arrived before him? How had she entered, unless she was one of the few who knew where to find the key? With her heart now torn between indignation and hurt, Flappy scampered over the frosted ground and pressed herself up against the wall beside the window. They had not bothered to close the curtains. The glow of the candles was dim, but bright enough for Flappy to see clearly were she to be fortunate enough to be given an opportunity. If they had gone upstairs, however, the opportunity would have been lost.

She edged towards the window. Then she slowly peered around the frame. It only took a moment. A brief glimpse was all she needed. A flash of scarlet, a second of recognition, a heartbeat of indignation. Briony! With her arms around Charles in a passionate embrace. How dare she!

Flappy was tempted to charge in and expose them. After all, Briony was her daughter-in-law! Charles had been her lover! The two of them together was more than she could stand. And yet, if Flappy was good at one thing, it was keeping a cool head when a cool head was required. Stifling a sob, because Flappy was mortified as well as angry, she backed away and retreated into the shadows of the garden. All the time she'd been thinking that Jasper was having an affair with Molly, Briony had been cheating on him with Charles. Flappy couldn't understand. Why would Charles have flirted with *her* if he was sleeping with Briony at the same time? It didn't make sense. Did he *want* to get caught? Surely he knew that Flappy would keep her word and meet him at the cottage. Or did he? Had it been a game? Had he suspected all along that Flappy was never going to give in? That Flappy was, deep down, a woman of honour and integrity. Then her heart deflated as the horrible realization dawned on her that she had been used as a decoy. She was the beard. An old and foolish beard! Oh, she had never felt more old and foolish than now. A deluded, pitiful woman, tricked into believing she was still young and beautiful and alluring. What a pathetic creature she was! Charles had toyed with her in order to divert Hedda, and perhaps even Flappy herself, from the truth: that he was having his wicked way with Briony. In that moment, when the light of honesty laid bare the extent of Flappy's delusions, she hated Briony and she hated Charles, but she hated neither as much as she hated herself.

Slowly and painfully she walked up the path towards the party. She wished she were Cinderella and that all the magic would turn to rags. She didn't want her *ballo in maschera* anymore. She didn't want to be the belle of the ball. She didn't want to be gracious and charming and beguiling. She wanted to find a hole, place herself in it, and drown in her tears.

Just then, a tall figure came hurrying down the path towards her, panting. Charles! Flappy stared at him as if he were a ghost. 'Darling, I'm so sorry!' he hissed breathlessly. 'I got stuck with Joan and you know—'

'Charles!' she exclaimed. Never before had she been so pleased to see him. She threw her arms around him and nuzzled his neck, clinging to him like a shipwrecked sailor clinging to a piece of driftwood. 'You're here!'

'Of course I am,' he replied, puzzled. He must have felt her tremble for he held her for a moment and then said, 'Are you all right?'

Flappy pulled away and looked up at him with a frown. 'But if you're here . . .' And then it struck her as if she'd been slapped in the face with a big wet fish. Of course. There was only one other man at the party dressed in a long black cloak - Jim. Now she understood why he had walked with such a cheery bounce in his step when she had seen him in town. Briony and Jim. Who'd have guessed it?

Charles put his hand in the small of her back. 'Come on, Beauty, we haven't a moment to lose and I'm as hot as a . . .' He hesitated, unable to think of a suitable simile.

But Flappy had come to her senses and her ardour had been extinguished. 'No,' she said, stepping away. She took off her mask. 'I'm sorry to have misled you, Charles. The excitement of the party got the better of me. You and I have had our moment. It's in the past and there we must leave it.'

'Because I was late?' he asked. He too took off his mask. He didn't look at all demonic now, just disappointed.

'No,' she said softly. 'Because I value the life I have too much to lose it. It's time we went back to the ball.'

Charles's shoulders dropped. He sighed. 'You're an enigma, Flappy,' he said, shaking his head in bewilderment.

'Would you at least like to dance with an enigma?' she asked, giving him a tender smile.

He smiled back, with resignation. 'Of course I would,' he replied. 'Who wouldn't want to dance with *you*?'

And as Flappy and Charles took to the dance floor, Flappy thought how ironic it was that Briony's infidelity had saved her from her own.

Chapter 16

The next morning Flappy awoke with a headache. It wasn't due to the champagne. She had, after all, only drunk one glass. No, it was due to the terrible discovery that Briony was having an affair. How long had it been going on for? she asked herself. Should she do something about it? She thought then of Tom and Jack, and Jasper and Molly, of course, and worried that if Briony and Jim decided they wanted to run off together, they'd break up not one but *two* families and shatter the happiness of *four* young children. Could they be that selfish?

Flappy was grateful that Kenneth had returned to their customary sleeping arrangements. Snoring away in his dressing room, Kenneth was oblivious to his wife's anxiety and the tossing and turning that had dogged her restless sleep. She got up and switched on the light. It was six o'clock. The ball had ended at two. Briony had left with Jasper, thanking Flappy for the fabulous evening without a hint of guilt upon her cheating lips. How could she have looked so serene, so innocent, after what Flappy had seen her do?

Flappy was nothing if not self-aware. She knew very well that she was not in a strong position to criticize her daughter-in-law. She'd had a brief affair with Charles, after all, and probably would have rekindled it had she not discovered Briony and Jim in the cottage. However, Charles and Hedda had an arrangement and Flappy certainly did not want to run off with him. She had only wanted sex. Did Briony want sex or did she want a whole new life?

Flappy opened the curtains. Outside, it was still night. Not even a distant glow could be seen breaking onto the horizon, for dawn was still a couple of hours away and all was still and quiet and deeply dark. She slipped into her dressing gown and went downstairs. She didn't feel like doing yoga or swimming this morning. She didn't even feel like a sauna. She wanted to sit quietly and think, and hope that a higher power would advise her on which course to take.

Many years before, an old Irishman had shared a slice of his wisdom, and the Irish were, Flappy thought, very wise. He'd said, when you want to say something, ask yourself these three questions: does it need to be said? Does it need to be said *now*? Are you the person to say it? As Flappy curled up in the big armchair in her green sitting room, she contemplated those three questions.

She thought hard and decided that it did *not* need to be said; it wasn't right to interfere in other people's lives, however badly they were behaving. Briony's infidelity was a matter for her and Jasper. If Flappy meddled, which, let us be clear, she never *ever* did unless she was left no alternative but to do so, she'd quite likely make it worse. If she left it, it might go away all on its own. The second question, whether it needed to be said *now*, was answered by the response to the first question. The final question, however, was more complicated. If it was going to be said at all then Flappy was, indeed, the right person to say it. No one else knew, as far as she could tell, and a quiet word in Briony's ear from her mother-in-law might just stop her in her tracks. Although, digging a little deeper into the question, Flappy feared that her interference might just make Briony and Jim more careful not to be detected. It might force them further underground. It might draw them closer together. It might even, heaven forbid, initiate their departure.

After a thorough analysis of the argument, she concluded that it was best to keep quiet, or rather, to keep her powder dry. She would observe the developments and come back to it at a later date. By then, the circumstances might have changed, for better or worse. Then, she might have to act, for the sake of her son.

Flappy's busy mind calmed somewhat. Her focus grew soft and her breathing slowed. In that moment of suspension an idea popped into her head. A brilliant idea. An idea so shrewd that Flappy was sure it had come from somewhere else. She sprang out of the armchair. She couldn't wait to tell Kenneth. She rolled up her dressing gown sleeve and looked at her watch. It was half past six. Kenneth wouldn't be up until nine, at least. Considering the time they went to bed, he might not be up until much later. There was nothing for it. With a skip now in her step and her thoughts as clear as crystal, she hurried down to the pool. She'd do an hour of yoga, half an hour of swimming and fifteen minutes in the sauna. Then she'd make herself breakfast.

When Kenneth finally emerged, his hair standing up in tufts, his dressing gown tied loosely over his belly and his feet in slippers, Flappy served him breakfast with a level of vigour that made him dizzy. 'Darling, you're very bouncy this morning,' he said, rubbing his eyes.

'It was a wonderful night,' she said happily.

'Yes, but I've got a headache,' he complained.

'That's what comes from drinking too much.'

'Still, it was fun, wasn't it? A huge success. You must be pleased. I don't think anyone will better it.' Kenneth knew very well how much his wife liked to be the best.

'It was splendid. Everyone had the most fabulous time.' Flappy brought him a cup of strong coffee and two fried eggs on toast. 'This will make you feel better.'

'You're a saint, thank you, darling,' said Kenneth, beginning to revive at the sight of food.

She sat down with a cup of tea with lemon and looked at him steadily. When Flappy wanted him to do something, she acquired a certain glint in her eyes. Kenneth frowned. 'Darling, I've got an idea,' she said, and her tone suggested that it was an important idea. The sort of idea that couldn't be ignored or put aside for later.

'Have you?' he asked, wondering how she could possibly be so alert after a heavy night and only a few hours' sleep. His head was full of fog.

'I think you should buy Jasper a house.'

Kenneth looked at her, his little eyes bright and alert suddenly. 'I thought you didn't want me to spoil him?' he said, confused.

'I've changed my mind. Now he's going to have a business to run, I'm feeling more generous towards him, and I do think he and Briony need a home of their own, rather than renting that cottage.'

'Really? I think they're happy there. It's next to the pub.'

'I think you should buy a derelict house which needs a great deal of work. The kind of house that will give Briony a project, something to do, for a very long time.'

'What's this about, Flappy?' Kenneth asked, sipping his cup of coffee. Kenneth recognized very well when Flappy's ideas had an ulterior motive to them.

Flappy narrowed her eyes and smiled, the smile of a cunning fox. 'I think Briony is bored. She's a bright girl with nothing to do. After all, they have an au pair to look after the children. What does she do with her time, I wonder?'

'Flappy?'

Flappy did not want to concern her husband with their daughter-in-law's infidelity, but she knew he was too intelligent not to sense that something was afoot. 'Let's just say she's got too much time on her hands. I'd like those hands to be busy. Very busy. Too busy to stray into areas where they ought not to be, if you get my drift.'

Kenneth's face darkened. His mind cleared of fog and he looked at her with a sharp and penetrating gaze. After all, it was not a foggy mind that had created a fast-food empire and sold it for millions. 'I hope you are very sure about what you are implying,' he said.

'I'm more than sure, darling. I *know*.'

'How serious is it?'

'That I *don't* know. But I need to ensure that it's nipped in the bud.'

'Then nipped in the bud it shall be.' Kenneth cut into his eggs on toast with vigour. 'Find me a house, Flappy, the most dilapidated house on the market, and I will do the rest. From what I know of Briony, a new house to do up and decorate will be just the thing to keep her entertained and busy, and diverted,' he added with emphasis.

'That's what I think,' Flappy agreed, reassured that Kenneth was taking control. What a team they were, the two of them. How could she ever have considered stealing into the cottage with Charles? She put a hand on his and squeezed it. 'You're one in a million, Toad,' she said, and as he smiled back at her, his eyes full of affection, he would never have imagined how close he had come to losing her.

It was a dazzling spring evening when Flappy and Kenneth stood beside Hedda and Charles and their many friends and acquaintances to celebrate the opening of Jasper and George. The sun was setting over the harbour, bouncing off the water in flashing spangles of light. The little boats, tethered to their moorings, gently rocked as the tide went out, and seabirds circled above the sand, diving to feast on the small crustaceans left behind by the retreating waves. It was an idyllic evening, made all the more so by the goodwill that enveloped the two young men as they opened their new restaurant to a community rooting for their success. Such were the people of Badley Compton, generous in their benevolence and willingness to support the two newcomers in their midst.

Flappy was proud of what Jasper had achieved. He had turned out to be a far shrewder businessman than she would have ever given him credit for. Perhaps there was more of his father in him than she had thought. The restaurant was stylish, thanks to her input. She, of course, would not have taken even an ounce of credit had the two young men not praised her in their speeches and thanked her for her advice. They said it had been 'invaluable'. Flappy knew very well exactly how much she had helped, and she had, it must be acknowledged, helped a great deal. But it was the boys' vision, ultimately, that had created the end result: a restaurant with the relaxed yet chic atmosphere of a venue in Mayfair, with a wholesome Mediterranean cuisine.

As sumptuous as the decor was, the food was key to its success and this is where Jasper and George had struck gold. The chef had come all the way from Sicily. A big, burly man with a thick head of curly brown hair, soft hazel eyes and the kind of charisma that one cannot acquire, however hard one might try. No, the charisma that Fulvio Belvedere had was a blessing bestowed on him at birth by a generous God. His presence filled the entire place and gave it a glamorous allure. His sex appeal was undeniable and Hedda, who had for some time been casting her eye about in search of an attractive man to entertain her, settled her roving gaze on him and it looked unlikely to rove any further.

Briony was thrilled with the ramshackle house that Kenneth had bought them. It was a few miles outside Badley Compton and needed a great deal of work. So much work, in fact, that it would have repelled a person of less ambition than Briony. But Briony had a vision, a wildly extravagant vision, to be sure, but a vision nonetheless that would tolerate no distraction. She was determined to transform it into a dream home. Nothing would divert her from her mission, and Flappy was pleased to see that her project gave her no time or desire for romantic dalliances. How did she know this, you might ask – well, Flappy was, by all accounts, a woman of devious means when devious means were required. She put her investigating talents to good use once again and discovered that Jim had turned his attention towards another pretty girl in town. But *she* was no concern of Flappy's. Molly, on the other hand, was. Flappy had grown fond of her, especially after she had painted such a ravishing portrait of Jasper. She decided, with typical generosity, to take the girl under her wing. What could be more considerate than personally advising her on her garden? After all, when it came to horticulture, no one knew plants and flowers better than Flappy. Molly would be so pleased.

Delighted that her own mission was complete, Flappy put away her binoculars and closed the drawer with a satisfied sigh. She wasn't one for self-congratulation, in fact self-congratulation was something in which she never *ever* indulged, it being so beneath her, but she couldn't help feeling, not for the first time, that she was so *so* lucky to have made the very good choices that she had.

One evening in June, Flappy was sitting alone on the terrace enjoying a moment's peace from her exceedingly demanding life, when she spotted a long-tailed skua on the lawn. Could it really be that elusive bird, she wondered, putting down her magazine. She was astonished. With its black cap and dark wings, white belly and very long tail, it was unmistakable, for Flappy had looked it up. She took off her sunglasses and watched it closely. In that rare moment of suspension, when her busy mind lay empty, a brilliant idea popped in. In fact, it was so brilliant it was one of her best. Flappy would paint the bird for Molly. It had been years since she had last taken out her brushes and watercolours, and, although she abhorred boasting, she had to admit that she really was rather good. In fact, if there was one thing Flappy was *very* good at, it was painting. Yes, she would paint the long-tailed skua for Molly. After all, it would be nothing for Flappy, but would mean so much to her new friend.

Flappy went inside to get her sketchpad and paints. There was no better time than the present because at every other moment she was so incredibly busy. She'd do it now, she decided, while she was inspired and while the bird was lingering on her lawn. As she returned to the garden a warm feeling expanded in her chest. There was no greater feeling than the one that came from doing something for someone else. Flappy was well acquainted with that feeling, being so thoughtful and giving. She settled down to paint and the warm feeling flowed onto the paper where the long-tailed skua gradually emerged in all its glory. Flappy gazed happily upon it and knew that it was good.

Acknowledgements

No one is more delighted that I have added a second novel to this new series than Flappy herself, although she always knew that I would. Ever since she appeared in *The Temptation of Gracie*, she has quite determinedly stolen the show. But even Flappy knows that the show would not be possible without the hard work, enthusiasm and skill of various exceptionally brilliant people who deserve our gratitude and appreciation. If there's one thing Flappy is good at, it's giving thanks where thanks is due.

Therefore, on behalf of Flappy and myself, I thank my agent, Sheila Crowley, and my editor, Suzanne Baboneau, who have given Flappy a global stage upon which to shine.

I am also grateful to my film agent, Luke Speed, and to all those at Curtis Brown who work on my behalf: Alice Lutyens, Sabhbh Curran and Emily Harris, Katie McGowan and Callum Mollison. A big thank you to Ian Chapman, my boss at Simon & Schuster, and his wonderful team who work so industriously and sensitively on my manuscripts: Sara-Jade

Virtue, Gill Richardson, Dominic Brendon, Polly Osborn, Rich Vlietstra, Sabah Khan, Matt Johnson, Francesca Sironi and Alice Rodgers.

I would also like to thank my husband, Sebag, our daughter Lily and our son Sasha for their support and encouragement and for finding Flappy as funny as I do. For every big, sweeping, emotionally charged novel that I write, a Flappy book is the perfect balm. And Flappy is thrilled that she makes me, and countless others, so happy. 'What sort of woman would I be if I kept my light all to myself?' she asks with typical humility, for such selfishness would be an abhorrence to Flappy. 'No, it is my duty and my delight to share it with the world. After all, it's really nothing for me and means so much to them.' And indeed, it does. Shine on, Flappy!

Santa Montefiore

Stories that stay

with you forever

Stay in touch with Santa for monthly updates
on her latest books.

Sign up for Santa's newsletter at
santamontefiore.co.uk

You can also connect with Santa on social media,
or follow her on Amazon for new book alerts.

🐦 SantaMontefiore

📷 SantaMontefioreOfficial

📘 /SantaMontefiorebooks

𝖆 bit.ly/FollowSanta

Discover more from *Sunday Times*
bestselling author Santa Montefiore ...

Flappy Entertains

'Fresh, fun and fabulous! Flappy certainly kept
me entertained!' HEIDI SWAIN

**Underneath her graceful exterior lies a passion nobody
knew about, least of all Flappy herself ...**

Flappy Scott-Booth is the self-appointed queen bee of
Badley Compton, a picturesque Devon village. While her husband
Kenneth spends his days on the golf course, she is busy overseeing
her beautiful house and gardens, and organising unforgettable
events, surrounded by friends who hang on to her every word.

Her life is a reflection of herself – impossibly perfect.

Until the day that Hedda Harvey-Smith and her husband Charles
move into the village. Into an even grander home than hers.
Taking the front seat on the social scene, quite literally.

That simply will not do.

Flappy is determined to show Hedda how things are done here in
Badley Compton. But then she looks into Charles's beautiful green eyes.
And suddenly, her focus is elsewhere. She is only human, after all ...

AVAILABLE NOW IN PAPERBACK, EBOOK AND EAUDIO

**SIMON &
SCHUSTER**